ANATOMY OF A SINGLE GIRL

ANATOMY OF A SINGLE GIRL

A NOVEL BY
DARIA
SNADOWSKY

DELACORTE PRESS

Text copyright © 2013 by Daria Snadowsky
Jacket photographs by Krister Engstrom
Digital imaging by Hothouse Designs

Visit us on the Web! randomhouse.com/teens

Educators and librarians, for a variety of teaching tools, visit us at RHTeachersLibrarians.com

Library of Congress Cataloging-in-Publication Data
Snadowsky, Daria.
Anatomy of a single girl / Daria Snadowsky.—1st ed.
p. cm.
Summary: "Sequel to Anatomy of a Boyfriend, in which college pre-med Dominique explores love and lust"—Provided by publisher.
ISBN 978-0-385-73798-2 (hc) — ISBN 978-0-375-89737-5 (ebook)
ISBN 978-0-385-90705-7 (glb)
[1. Dating (Social customs)—Fiction. 2. Sex—Fiction. 3. Universities and colleges—Fiction.
4. Florida—Fiction.] I. Title.
PZ7.S664953Ap 2013
[Fic]—dc23
2012012186

The text of this book is set in 12-point Apollo MT.
Book design by Angela Carlino

Printed in the United States of America

10 9 8 7 6 5 4 3 2 1

First Edition

FOR J—

WITH LOVE

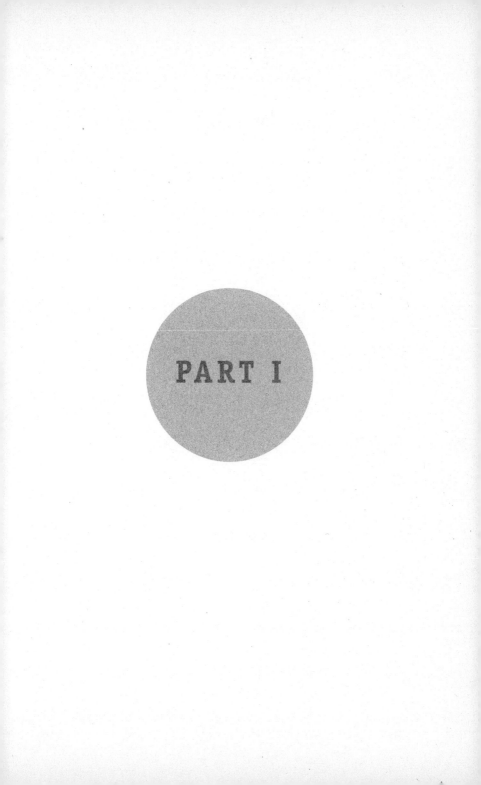

PART I

The logical thing would be for me to date Calvin Brandon.

For starters, he's one of the nicest people I know at Tulane (or anywhere else). Unlike most college guys, he doesn't need Budweiser, ESPN, or an Xbox to survive. We always have fun together and can totally be ourselves around each other. And no matter how frazzled I got by my summer electives, which crammed a semester's worth of biology into only May and June, he could still make me laugh. On top of all that, Calvin *explicitly* told me that he'd like me to be his girlfriend.

I'd be the luckiest girl in Louisiana to be his girlfriend. . . .

So why don't I *want* to be his girlfriend?

I'm trying not to obsess about it, when a plane taking off suddenly whooshes over the New Orleans airport, where Calvin's keeping me company on the curbside baggage-check line. The loud rumbling of the engines forces us to stop talking. But while we stand there in silence, staring at each other, the mood turns awkward as we surely have the same thought: what a perfect moment for a first kiss. But as I *explicitly* told Calvin, I'm not interested in dating anyone right now.

But maybe it's that I'm not interested in dating *him* right now.

Or perhaps I'm not interested in dating him *ever*?

So much for not obsessing about it.

I break the tension by taking out my cell phone and logging on to the university registrar. Once the engine noise lifts, Calvin glances at the display and says, "Professors don't have to submit grades until sometime in July, you know. There's no way anything's posted yet."

"It never hurts to double-check. I'm going crazy waiting for results."

"You have nothing to worry about, Coppertone," he declares, using his favorite new nickname for me. It's meant to poke fun at my red hair (hence "copper") as well as the vast amounts of sunblock I go through (to keep my fair, freckle-prone skin from becoming red, too). "I bet you aced everything. You hit the books harder than all of the other freshmen combined—"

"Hold it right there. I'm officially a rising *sophomore*, Mr. Know-It-All Rising Senior. And those were the toughest finals of my life, so all bets are off."

4

"At least you're a few credits ahead now. And you know what that means. Extra free time to spend with me next year!" He flashes an openmouthed smile.

"Ha ha," I murmur, ignoring his thinly veiled come-on. Although Calvin has assured me he's okay with keeping things platonic, he hasn't stopped dropping suggestive hints. It's annoying . . . and a little flattering. Who doesn't like being liked?

Soon we near the front of the line, and as I'm rummaging through my backpack for my ID, he says, "You realize it's still not too late to forget this Fort Myers madness, don't you? That's the biggest perk of being eighteen, Coppertone—you're no longer obligated to follow your parents' orders."

I roll my eyes. "Going home is *my* choice, Cal. Second-year premed's supposed to be brutal, and I don't want to burn out on school before it even starts. Anyway, the deadline to enroll in the last summer session was yesterday."

"You don't have to take any more classes here. Just work at Res-Life with me! We could use help in the office manning the phones."

"Hmm." I patter my fingers on my chin in feigned contemplation. "As much as I'd love to spend the rest of break fielding drunken calls about lost room keys, I'm sticking with Florida."

"Fine! Pass up a boring desk job for palm trees and piña coladas. *Be that way,*" he huffs, which just makes us both break out in giggles.

After my luggage gets checked, Calvin walks me the few steps to the terminal entrance and asks, "So, any exciting plans for the Fourth next weekend, without me?"

I explain how I'll be with my best friend, Amy, whose mom and stepdad always invite me to their family barbecue. "And how about you, Cal? Chaperoning some lame coed mixer on the Riverwalk?"

"Dunno. I'll probably just cloister myself in my single, research MBA programs, and explore a life of solitude and self-reflection."

I roll my eyes again. "Well, despite your *im*moral support, it was very cool of you to come and help with my bags. I know move-out days are über-busy for you Res-Lifers, so thank you."

I'm expecting him to dish out another wiseass remark. Instead, he turns toward me and says solemnly, "Thank *you* for letting me drag you out of the library once in a while. These last two months have been awesome. I really wish you were staying, Dominique."

I don't think I've ever been so startled to hear my name before, and I definitely wasn't prepared for him to lay on the mushiness. In an attempt to deflect it, I answer, "Oh, next semester is just around the corner, and once I'm back, you'll get sick of me."

But he doesn't seem to listen as his piercing brown eyes lock me into their gaze. As I let myself gaze at him, too, I think how Amy is so correct that a good personality can make a guy better-looking. Back in the fall when Calvin was an RA in my dorm, I could barely distinguish him from every other medium-height, middleweight Average Joe roaming the halls. Then again, the more he flirted with me, the more I wrote him off as a drip. It wasn't until the end of spring term, when we were two of the only undergrads not leaving campus, that I accepted his hail on IM and promptly realized how blind I'd been. We began hanging out, and, like magic, he grew more attractive with every laundry run, gym workout, and team trivia game we did together. And at this moment, with his dimpled cheeks ruddy from the 80 percent humidity and his bushy eyebrows squinty from the afternoon sun, he's downright adorable. . . .

So why don't *I* adore him?

Or am I not *letting* myself adore him?

Or what if—

Just then, another plane zooms overhead, and engine buzz again drowns out all conversation in the loading zone. Calvin's still staring me down, and I catch him licking his lips. A few feet away from us, there's a couple Frenching each other goodbye, sex-ifying the ambience even more. Suddenly some tourist bounding out of her cab accidentally sideswipes my backpack, causing me to fall forward against Calvin's left shoulder. Instantly, his hands grip my waist, steadying me. It's like the universe is commanding us, *Thou shalt suck face!*

But the next thing I know, I'm pushing away from him.

"Sorry," I say, flustered, when the rumbling subsides. "Lost my balance there for a sec."

"You hurt?"

"Oh, no. I'm fine." I hold up my wristwatch and pretend to check the time. "Wow, I'd really better motor. And you, too. The shuttle back should be leaving any minute."

Calvin nods sluggishly, clearly disappointed by what just didn't happen. But he bucks up and nudges my upper arm with his knuckles. "All righty, Coppertone. Have a safe trip and an awesome vacation. You certainly earned a breather from this place."

"Thanks, Cal. I will."

7

"And, hey—I get that it's easy to lose touch when everyone's away doing their own thing, and I promise not to pester you. But this is your home now, too, so try not to fall completely off the face of the earth, okay?"

"I won't, and you *don't* pester me."

"Cool. And beware of strange guys on your plane. They're just interested in a one-*flight* stand."

I grin. "Yeah, 'cause I'm *really* the mile-high-club type."

Calvin's grinning, too, and I sigh in relief that we've eased back into our normal repartee. Then I slide my boarding pass into my jeans pocket and say, "Well . . . um . . . see ya."

"See ya, Coppertone."

I head toward the sliding glass doors, but I can sense Calvin still standing there watching me, and I know this can't be the end. Even though we're just friends, he's become the most special person to me at school, and he deserves something more than "See ya." So I do a quick one-eighty, sprint back, and embrace him as tightly as I can. He wraps his arms around me, too, and it feels so comfy and peaceful. Finally we exchange a round of smiles and waves before I go inside for real, this time more than pleased with how we're leaving things. Hugs are really underrated.

Sure I'm curious what kissing him would be like, and I've always wanted to experience one of those romantic airport farewells. But it would've been unfair of me to blur the line between us prior to parting for eight weeks, when the kiss would've meant more to him than to me. Besides, it was already major progress just deliberately getting that physically close to any guy other than my ex-boyfriend.

2

There's no doubt that I won the parents lottery in all the really important respects. And as much as I love college, I still get homesick for our family fishing boat trips, which we've taken almost every Sunday for as long as I can remember. Nonetheless, when I find my parents waiting for me at the Fort Myers airport baggage claim that evening, donning matching TULANE MOM and TULANE DAD T-shirts and baseball caps, I want to run in the opposite direction.

"So sue us if we're proud," Dad responds to my grimace. "It's not every day our only child finishes her first year *plus* extra summer courses at a world-class university."

"Welcome back, future Dr. Baylor!" Mom proclaims

during our group hug. "Goodness me, you've really slimmed down since spring break!" Then she taps my hips with both hands and fixes her eyes right on my backside as if this isn't one of the most embarrassing things she could do to me in public. "Yes, Dommie, you're just like your old self again!"

"'*Old* self'?" Dad parrots. "Dom looks *better than ever!*"

I didn't expect to get school-sick this soon. I know they mean well, though, so I just grin and bear it until we arrive home to our apartment and Amy drives over. After my parents fuss over her as well for finishing her first year at Amherst College and making the track team, Amy and I take sanctuary in my bedroom, where I bring her up to date.

"So let me get this straight," she says while helping me unpack. "You're not in love with Calvin, but you *wish* you were in love with Calvin?"

"All I mean is that it'd be really convenient if I were, because we'd be a perfect couple!"

"Dom, there's no such thing," Amy gripes as I hand her old binders to shelve in my desk hutch. "After the first few months and the honeymoon period fizzles out, even good relationships become dull and routine."

"Whatever. That's just another way of saying 'stable' and 'committed,' which is the whole point of being in a good relationship to begin with."

"Yeah, yeah." Amy slumps her shoulders and sighs. "But it's really no coincidence that 'monogamy' sounds just like 'monotony.'"

In the neuroscience course I just took, my textbook said that sex drive is regulated in an area of the brain's hypothalamus that's about the size of a cherry. But with Amy

Braff, who's always been able to—and did—hook up with any boy her hormones desired, it's probably closer to the size of a grapefruit. So no one was more shocked than Amy when she fell hard for fellow fine arts major Joel Wagner during Amherst's freshman orientation and started dating him exclusively. Considering he's the only boy Amy's ever cared for enough to go all the way with, she assumed they could handle a summer apart while he teaches ceramics at his old camp in Kansas and she interns at the Rauschenberg Gallery here in Florida. Summer's barely half over, though, and Amy's back to her old ways of lusting after every cute guy who enters her field of vision.

"There's 'water, water everywhere, and not a drop to drink,'" she sings mournfully while we nest my emptied suitcases inside each other.

"It's just a hunch, Ames, but I don't think Joel would feel too happy to know you're talking like this."

"Joel should feel *honored*." Amy squeezes the gold heart locket necklace that he bought her fall semester. "That I'm willing to endure this torment for him *proves* our love is real."

I sigh and smile at her classic Amy twisted logic. "Well, whatever works."

"Anyway, I'm still allowed to look but not touch, like at an art gallery show. And on the subject of boy-watching"— she pulls off her hair band and shakes out her ebony locks— "we're late for our next engagement!"

After I hug my parents goodbye and remind them I'll be sleeping over at the Braffs', Amy drives us to a kegger at a Cape Coral loft that some of the other Rauschenberg interns are subletting together. This is my first Saturday night all summer of not studying, so it's great just kicking back and meeting everyone Amy's been talking about for the last two months. I'm not sad once the party ends, though, because it means I get Amy to myself again. We haven't seen each other since February, when she visited me at school for Mardi Gras.

"Sorry," Amy says after we get back into her Camry, this time with me in the driver's seat. "I shouldn't have asked you to be the DD."

"Hey, I'm used to it, and I still had fun," I assure her while pulling out onto the street.

"But then you could've let loose more. I just couldn't resist those Jell-O shots!"

"Well, no judgment, Ames, but Jell-O shots were the least of what you couldn't 'resist' back there." I raise an eyebrow at her, and Amy scrunches her forehead, genuinely confused, before catching on.

"I was just giving Zack a back rub! Everyone does that for each other at work. You get sore lugging around canvases all day."

"Okay, but how about that Stefan guy?"

"What? We were dancing!"

"Yeah, but you were all smushed up against him. Have you forgotten your whole 'look but don't touch' rule?"

"Stop! You're killing my buzz!" Amy clamps her hands over her ears. Then she decrees, "Fine. The rule's amended: I can 'touch but not tongue.'"

"Yeah, keep telling yourself that," I say through my laughter.

Back during Mardi Gras while Amy was staying with

me, my hall-mates couldn't figure out how she and I ever became close, since we have virtually nothing in common besides being five foot six. The truth is, it all stems from having alphabetical seating in our tiny sixth-grade class. Our *B* last names guaranteed that we would always be adjacent and get coupled up for projects, so it was only a matter of time before we bonded. I also appreciated how she never teased me about my mother working as a math teacher at our school. That may have been a return favor for my never making cracks about *her* mother being a well-known psychotherapist specializing in sex issues. I worried about what would happen in ninth grade, when Amy fled to a big public school and I stayed behind in private, but we continued to think of each other as the sister we'd never had. That was why I didn't worry at all in twelfth grade when we weren't interested in any of the same colleges.

"Now, enough about *moi*," Amy croons. "Whom among the male selection back there could *you* see breaking your self-imposed celibacy with?"

I shrug apathetically.

"C'mon, Dom. I was banking on vicariously getting with at least one boy through you this summer."

"So *that's* why you asked me to come tonight," I say with another eyebrow raise.

"Seriously, you can't imagine wanting *any* of those guys?"

"I didn't feel a spark. Not that it matters, since none of them seemed to, either. At least Cal was into me from the beginning."

"Oh, him again." Amy stretches out in the passenger seat. "Your friend with*out* benefits."

"Very funny."

Suddenly my phone beeps in my purse, and Amy checks it for me.

"Speak of the devil . . ." She clears her throat before reciting Calvin's text in a mock-excited voice. " 'Hi, Coppertone! Hope all is well in sunny FL. Just wanted to say goodnight.' Aw, that's really nice!"

"Can you write back for me 'Sweet dreams'?"

Amy smirks naughtily. "Sure . . . but can I leave out the first *s* and an *e*?"

"Huh?" I picture it in my mind: *Wet dreams.* "Ames, don't you dare! The only reason my friendship with him works is because I *never* lead him on!"

"Okay. Calm down. Don't have a conniption!"

After texting my reply, Amy scrolls through my photos of Audubon Aquarium, where Calvin took me as a surprise yesterday to celebrate the end of my exams. Then, as I'm pulling into the Braffs' driveway, she drops the phone back into my purse and says, "My, my. The Cal-man really looks stuck on you. Poor guy."

"Well, we still might get together at some point."

"Dom." Amy scowls. "You. Don't. Like. Him. That. Way. End. Of. Story."

"But maybe I *would've* liked him that way if I'd met him, like, tonight instead of back in October. Let's face it. I wasted freshman year clinging to *you know who,* and then reeling from the damage when we went up in smoke, so I was *not* in a receptive head space. Maybe Cal was just a victim of bad timing."

"You sound like my mom."

"And Cal and I now have a strong foundation to develop something more serious."

"I'm sorry—did you say you wanted a boyfriend or a building?"

"Go ahead, make fun. But I'm treating this vacation as a kind of experiment. If I end up missing Cal a lot, that could mean there *is* relationship potential between us and I just haven't been ready to see him as more than a friend. I know it's a long shot, but I want to be open to the possibility."

"Uh-huh. Well, if the possibility becomes an actuality, will you greet him with a smooch when he picks you up at the airport? Aah! I'd *so* pay admission to see his face!"

"Please. The boy just dropped me off, and you're talking about the end of August, so I think we're jumping the gun." I chuck her the car keys and grab my overnight bag before we trot up the front path to her house. "And whatever happens, I'm glad Cal and I have a break from each other. That whole situation was getting stressful."

"Well, you've come to the right place," Amy cheers, swinging open the front door and ushering me inside. "Now that you're back, prepare to *de*-stress, starting now!"

During those next few hours, Amy and I practically regress to the tweens we once were as we reenact our first sleepover nearly eight years ago—singing along to *Grease*, playing Marco Polo in her pool, moon-bathing in her yard, giving each other manicures, and chattering until the Sunday dawn. Unfortunately, I wake up too late to join my parents for fishing, but it was worth it just finally getting to hang out with my best friend again without phones or computer screens between us. That's another reason why I decided not to remain in New Orleans all summer—so Amy and I could rack up more quality girl-time before another long school year of being seven states apart. It never occurs to me that her boyfriend could get in the way.

3

Thursday morning I'm chaining my bike behind Lee County Medical, where I've started a volunteer internship for the summer, when Amy calls to break the news: Joel said during their video chat date last night that he found her a discount airfare for a round-trip flight from Fort Myers to Wichita.

"It's some special Independence Day weekend rate," she explains. "There's a red-eye leaving here tonight, and the return flight is Sunday afternoon."

I feel like my cell phone just stung me in the ear. "Isn't Joel going to be busy at camp?"

"Yeah, but he has breaks throughout the day, and lights-out is from ten to six."

"You said he lives in a bunk with other counselors, though. So how could you two even . . . *you know*?"

"We can pitch a tent in the woods and light a fire. Joel says that's what the other couples do."

"But your parents' barbecue is tomorrow."

"So? It'll be boring, as usual."

"Oh." I take a seat on the curb and pout.

I want to point out how Amy will be seeing Joel just next month when he flies in for her stepbrother, Matt's, wedding. And we already made plans this weekend for more retro girlie "play dates" like Glamour Shots at Edison Mall, home facials, and of course another sleepover. But then I recall last summer when I was in Amy's shoes and how she never complained about being only my second-choice person to spend time with. That's just the reality of having a best friend who's also someone's girlfriend—you have to share.

I force myself to sound supportive. "This is beyond romantic, Ames! He's clearly really pining for you, and you've clearly been really, um—"

"Horny?"

"*Actually,* I was about to say 'restless,' but sure." We both laugh. "So I guess we'll just see each other when you get back on Sunday."

"You didn't think I was gonna up and desert you, did you? You should totally come away with me, too! My mom's letting me use her credit card, which has plenty of points to cover our airfare."

"Oh . . . well, that's awesome of you and your mom and everything, but what would *I* do at your boyfriend's camp?"

"Hike on their trails, swim in their lake, and Joel said we can use the dining hall. It'll be a blast just chilling out!"

"I don't know, Ames. This is really last-minute. Plus I have two bratsitting gigs later today, so I'd be rushing to pack."

"*Please?* If you come, I can hang with you *and* my man. And it's high time you two met."

"What about sleeping arrangements?"

"Joel will get an extra cot for you in the girl counselors' bunkhouse. Unless, of course, you hit it off with one of the guy counselors and you camp out there yourselves," she says coyly.

"Yeah, 'cause *that's* likely." I get back on my feet and make for the hospital employee entrance. "Listen, the logistics sound too complicated, and I don't want to be a third wheel anyway. Forget about me, and I'll just meet Joel at Matt's wedding."

After a beat, Amy mutters, "I feel horrible flaking out on you, Dom. Say the word, and I'll nix the whole trip."

I smile because I know she means it, but I also know I shouldn't stand in her way, so I promise her that everything's cool. Then later, when my supervisor begs me to come in for the overnight shift tomorrow since the holiday is leaving them short-staffed, it seems that everything has worked out for the best.

As far as the Braffs' barbecue, I opt to go for three reasons: One, Dr. Braff calls to reassure me that I'm always welcome there with or without her daughter. Two, there's nothing happening at my place since Dad, the local chief of police, is needed at headquarters because the Fourth is a high crime night, and Mom will be there, too, helping the desk sergeants manage the increased call volume. And three, I assumed Amy was exaggerating when she warned me about Matt's fiancée, Brie, becoming the most irritating person on the planet.

I never got to know Brie well. The few other times I've seen her have been at past Braff get-togethers, and she and Matt typically kept to themselves. They graduated from college in May, though they've been dating since their junior year of high school, so we all expected it when Matt popped the question last Valentine's Day. I'm excited because I've never been to a wedding before, and it'll be twice as fun going to one with Amy there as a bridesmaid. But as Brie blathers on all evening about centerpieces, personalized napkins, embossed place cards, and gift registries, I understand why Amy escaped to another state. I also have a newfound respect for my parents' decision twenty years ago to elope with no fanfare at Fort Myers City Hall.

"Did you get your invitation yet?" Brie asks me after Dr. Braff goes into the kitchen to make more punch, leaving us alone on the porch. "Each one was hand-calligraphed with a real wax seal!"

"Yep, came in the mail yesterday. It was beautiful!" I pretend to rave, struggling to keep my eyes from glazing over. I'd like to escape inside, too, but it'd be rude to ditch Brie while she's still having dinner. Part of her pre-wedding diet regimen includes taking painfully long pauses between bites to trick herself into feeling fuller with less food.

"I can't believe I'll be a wife in only forty-three days!" she peals after blowing a kiss to Matt in the backyard, where he's playing glow-in-the dark badminton with his dad. "We're so thrilled you'll be able to share our big day with us!"

"Aw. Well, thank you so much for including me."

"You're welcome! I know you're practically family here, which means soon *we'll* be family. And I've been wanting to ask you . . ." She sips her vitaminwater. "Will you be bringing a date?"

"Doesn't look like it," I drone, now wishing I'd been rude.

"What about that guy you were here with last Fourth of July?"

I'm prepared for this. One of the pitfalls of having an ex-boyfriend is that people still pair you together in their memories, and sooner or later someone's bound to mention him. And now that it has happened . . . I can't say I feel nothing. I don't think it's possible to get royally dumped by the only boy I've ever done it with, let alone loved, and then feel nothing when he's brought up in conversation. This whole recovery process has been two steps forward, one step back, but I feel okay. I've *been* feeling okay. And that's pretty incredible, considering that just this past February, on the very day Brie was being proposed to, merely the word "valentine" reduced me to tears.

"We split over Christmas break," I state matter-of-factly.

I'm *not* prepared for what comes next. From the way Brie's jaw hits the table, you'd guess I just told her I have three months to live.

"Oh, Dominique. No!" She gulps down the half-masticated vegan burger sludge still in her mouth. "When you didn't bring him tonight, I was afraid that might've been why, but . . . I could've sworn you two were forever! Oh, what a shame, you poor, poor girl!"

Doesn't she realize that's the most demoralizing reaction to breakup news ever? All my school friends said stuff along the lines of, *Hooray for moving on to bigger and better things!* They may not have meant it, but it was nicer to hear.

"Thanks, Brie, but like I said, it's been ages."

I take out my cell phone to check e-mail, not caring that it's impolite. I'm assuming the subject's closed. I assume wrong.

"Now, I faintly remember him talking about how he was planning to major in English. Did he go to Tulane also?"

I sigh. "NYU."

"*Thaaat's* right. And you two didn't go to the same high school here, either."

Is that a question?

"Correct. He went to Amy's."

"So you met through her?"

"Um . . . sorta . . ."

I sigh again, recollecting that winter's day senior year when Amy took me to her school's charity football game. Like a dolt, I tripped on my way to a Porta Potti, and *he* happened to be nearby and helped me up. There were instant sparks, but we were both shy, and it took two agonizing months of friendship before he worked up the guts to confess he wanted more. The moment we got together still ranks as the most magical in my life, though I should've taken the Porta Potti as a sign of where things would end up. It seems impossible that that football game was a year and a half ago. I remember it more vividly than this morning. But I'm not about to trot out the humiliating details for Brie's sake.

"Actually," I continue, "I probably never would've met

him if it weren't *for* Amy, but she wasn't close friends with him or anything. They just knew each other from both being on the track team."

"Oh, okay. It's coming back to me now. He'd mentioned he was a sprinter—well, he certainly had a runner's body."

I don't respond.

"So tell me"—Brie clucks before taking another micro-bite of her bun-less burger—"what happened with you guys?"

I have to stop myself from asking if she's for real. Brie has barely ever bothered to speak to me before today. So nothing entitles her to know that my ex-boyfriend, who had sworn his undying love to me during our last semester of high school, ceased having feelings for me during our first semester of college. She has no right to hear how he wanted to stay friends but that I wasn't about to reward his change of heart by being demoted to a pal. And it's no one's business that he and I haven't communicated since, and chances are we never will. But because it'd be awkward for a wedding guest to tell the bride to quit acting like a nosy bitch, I stick to vagueness. "It just seemed smart to keep our options open since we were so far away from each other."

"Omigod, Dom, I know *exactly* what you mean! It was really hard at first with Matt in Ithaca and me at Bennington, but I'm so relieved we resolved to make it work. I couldn't imagine a future without him now." Brie extends her left arm and grins goofily at her 1.67-carat princess-cut solitaire before blowing another kiss at Matt. Then she gapes, wide-eyed, at me. "But there must be a chance of a reconciliation. I hate the thought of anyone being dateless at my wedding."

I'm brainstorming how to respond to that without telling Brie to shove her ring where the sun don't shine, when fireworks suddenly explode over San Carlos Bay, prompting us all to drop everything and scuttle to the front lawn for a better view. I'm grateful for the interruption, though the pang in my chest indicates it's too late. The wound's been torn open.

I'd been looking forward to the fireworks all day. Now I hardly notice them as I replay in my head Brie gagging on the word "dateless" as if it were code for "pathetic hopeless ugly reject." Like I haven't wasted enough time feeling like one. Then when I realize that everybody's paired up— Amy's mom on her husband's lap on the porch swing, and Brie on Matt's lap on a patio chair—it dawns on me that I'm a *fifth* wheel. Inevitably my mind begins wandering where it shouldn't: *At this precise moment last year in this same spot, I was on someone's lap as well. . . . I wonder if anyone's on his lap now. . . .*

I mentally slap myself across the face and keep my eyes trained on the sky, in a futile attempt to focus on the present. Perhaps I should've joined Amy in Kansas after all, though she's probably sitting on Joel's lap now, too—or going down on it, more likely. I consider texting Calvin for an ego boost, but seeking out the one boy who wants me, just so I can vent about another boy who doesn't, would be irredeemably dumb. And cruel. Bitching about the past never helps anyway.

I don't have to report to the hospital for another two hours, but I've learned from experience that the best way to combat "steps back" is to lose myself in work as quickly as possible. So the instant the fireworks end, I announce that I need to get to my internship. Soon I'm racing away on my bike, wishing I had never come in the first place.

Fortunately, my supervisor keeps me plenty busy throughout my shift, and before I know it, I'm lumbering to the cafeteria to refuel on yogurt and granola for the ride home. I'm feeling okay again. Or maybe I'm too drained to feel anything after pulling an all-nighter of unpacking medical supplies, digitizing files, operating the switchboard, and fetching coffee for the staff. Whatever the case, the crisis is averted, and all I'm thinking is how good it will be to snooze away the Saturday.

I finish eating and am gearing up to leave, when one of the hottest guys I've ever seen sits down opposite me at the next table.

PART II

4

His cell phone starts ringing as soon as he pulls in his chair.

"Hey, dude," he answers lethargically. "Yeah, Bruce will be fine. Just his forearm got burned, and the doctor said it's only second-degree . . ."

Next to my tray is a back issue of *Scientific American* I borrowed from the waiting room to skim during breakfast. As a reflex, I hold it up and pretend to keep reading so I can sneakily observe him over the top of the pages.

". . . I think we can safely assume he'll never go near another firecracker again. . . ."

He looks older than me, but not by much.

". . . We were here five hours before they finally took him in, so I couldn't sleep, 'cause I was constantly bringing him wet paper towels from the bathroom. . . ."

He's smokin', all right—square jaw, Greek nose, full lips, slight tan.

". . . Then he kept sobbing about what a good friend I was to stay with him. To get even for everything, I'm gonna make him do my laundry for a month. . . ."

But he's cuddly, too, courtesy of his apple cheeks and dimpled chin.

". . . At the desk, they said this was the busiest they've been since New Year's. Guess Bruce wasn't the only dickwad playing with pyrotechnics last night. . . ."

And his hair's a fluffy jumble of sand-colored ringlets that shoot out every which way in a kind of 'fro.

". . . Yeah, he's all gauzed up now, in one of those curtained ER rooms, so I'm just grabbing some food. . . ."

Like me, he has green eyes, although his are a lot paler, resembling mint ice cream. They're almost incandescent under the fluorescent lighting.

". . . We can go once a nurse comes to remove his IV, which they said should be around nine, so not much longer. . . ."

I like how he's built and broad-shouldered without crossing the line into gross muscleman territory.

". . . Don't sweat it, dude. I'm here, so I might as well take him home, too. You sound too hungover to drive anyhow. . . ."

And from the way his torso towers above the table and his outstretched legs extend out from under it, he can't be any less than six two.

". . . Oh, and tell the guys we have to remember to get a new fire extinguisher. . . . Okay, see ya soon."

I'm not sure what I hope to accomplish by sticking around. If Amy were in my place, she wouldn't think twice about striking up a conversation with this guy. But I've never been able to make a move like that. Either way, it's superficial of me to want us to meet, when I probably wouldn't have noticed him if he weren't nice eye candy.

I must be doing a lousy job of acting inconspicuous, because all of a sudden he returns my stare. In a flash I resume reading, though I'm blushing from having been caught checking him out. This would be a good time to make my exit, but a few seconds later I find myself stealing another peek, and he's *still* looking at me. We both drop our gazes, and I feel a little less stalker-ish, since I caught him checking me out as well. After another pause, I glance at him once more, and he's furtively peering at me while keeping his head bowed, so I look away again. It's like we're playing footsie with our eyes.

"That's my favorite magazine," I hear him say.

My insides constrict as I slowly lift my nose from the page to face him.

"Really?" I squeak. "Your favorite?"

"Uh-huh. Actually, it's a tie between that and *Wired*."

"Cool. . . . Did you want it?" I hold out the magazine to him, and dorkily add, "It's hospital property, so just make sure not to go home with it."

"No need. I already read that one, but thanks."

A lull ensues as he looks back down at his tray and begins spreading cream cheese on his bagel. Now that the ice is broken, I know if I leave, I'll just wonder what might have been. I'm scrambling for something to talk about, but he speaks first.

"So, how long have you been volunteering?"

"Oh . . . just since Monday. How did you know I worked here?"

His forehead wrinkles. "Well, I kinda inferred." He gestures to my scrubs and necklace tag, which bears the word "volunteer" in big block letters. Duh.

"Right. My normal hours are nine to three during the week, but I helped out last night for the Fourth and just got off duty . . . and so did my brain."

My cheeks flush again, but he gives me a comforting smile. Even his teeth are perfect.

"That's nothing," he says. "*My* brain's so fried that at the drinks station just now, I poured orange juice into my Cheerios instead of milk. I had to throw the whole thing out."

I crack up laughing. Not because it's funny. I'm just so pleased to see someone cute being kind as well. Cuteness and kindness are often inversely proportional in people. Then I tell him, "I overheard what you said, by the way. I'm sorry about your friend. But if it's just a second-degree burn, he'll blister but might not scar."

"Yeah, it didn't look that serious." He starts in on his second bagel slice. "Normally I'd have just hauled him to Student Health, but it's closed on the weekends until fall."

At that, my ears perk up even more. "Oh, you go to college around here?"

He nods. "Ford."

"Henry Ford Institute of Technology?" I beam. "When I was in high school, they let me audit a human anatomy class, and I was going to apply there, too. But then I decided I should try out a different city since I'd lived here my whole life."

"I hear that. Georgia Tech would've been my first choice if my family weren't in Atlanta."

He polishes off the rest of the bagel, and I'm afraid he's going to return to Bruce now. Instead he smacks his lips and asks, "So, what school *did* you go to?"

Within five minutes he has abandoned his chair for the one across from me at my table. I discover that he's nineteen, is going to be a junior, has declared a physics major, and rooms with Bruce in their fraternity house—Beta Zeta Phi. Mostly, though, we discuss his summer work as a research apprentice helping to devise new ways to isolate neutrons. Yeah. Cuteness and intelligence don't frequently coexist, either, so he's an exception to that, too. Only a half hour elapses from the time we first speak to when Bruce texts him that he's being wheeled out, but there's no question that I'm drawn to this guy for a lot more than his looks.

"I guess I should bring my car around," he tells me after messaging back Bruce. "Sorry for talking shop so much. My Beta brothers would've told me to shut up by now."

"Are you kidding? I'm just jealous you get to do actual science for your job when my work here's all secretarial. I want to know more."

"Yeah?" He grins. "That could be arranged. . . . We should swap numbers and stuff."

"Yeah, sure." I try not to say it too eagerly, though I'm euphoric that he took the bait.

We bump phones over the table, and it's only after they

sync that I realize we've never actually introduced ourselves.

"So, you're Dominique Lilith Baylor?" he reads from his
display. "Cool name."

"Thanks, but everyone calls me Dom. It was after my
grandpa Dominic. And 'Lilith,' my parents chose because in
mythology she was, like, this infamous feminist redhead—"

"Oh, yeah. Lilith was Adam's wife before Eve, but she
left the Garden of Eden because she refused to be subservi-
ent to Adam." I must appear impressed, because he shrugs
and goes on, "I took religion last year for a distribution
requirement."

Fighting my compulsion to kiss him for sounding so
erudite, I look down at my own cell. "And you're . . . Guy
Davies?"

"Uh-huh. There's no significance behind 'Guy,' though.
My mom and dad just weren't very imaginative."

I smile and reach out my hand to him. "Well, *I* like it.
Nice to meet you, Guy."

He squeezes my hand as we shake, unleashing a swarm
of butterflies beating against my abdomen. I haven't had that
in so long, and I love how transcendent it feels—like I'm
weightless, or free-falling through space. It lasts for only a
second, though, before the past flashes before my eyes and I
fill with dread.

Now I'll be spending the next who-knows-how-many
days waiting for Guy to call/text/IM/Facebook/e-mail me.
Then, *if* he ever does, I'll devote who-knows-how-many
hours to reading into every word and deliberating about
how to respond so I come off as available but not clingy. We

may call/text/IM/Facebook/e-mail back and forth for who-knows-how-much longer until we start hanging out, *if* we ever do. Meanwhile I'll keep scrutinizing his behavior for signs as to whether he wants me romantically or as just a friend, and my mood will yo-yo accordingly until he finally makes a move, *if* he ever does.

I used to think all that game playing was par for the course and even kind of exciting. It just felt logical to pursue a boy the same way I applied to college—by expending exorbitant time and energy showing what a great catch I am and what a perfect match we'd be, so that after a lengthy waiting period I might get accepted. But now the idea of reliving any version of that charade seems like hell. It's also pointless, considering that the connection between Guy and me is undeniable. That is, I *think* it is. I doubt he would've started talking to me, moved seats, and asked for my contact information if he weren't at least *interested* in being interested in me. . . .

But maybe he was just being polite.

Maybe he already has a girlfriend.

Why *wouldn't* someone like him have a girlfriend?

But, then, why is he squeezing my hand?

He could just have a firm grip—

I'm sick of always second-guessing!

"Would you like to do something tonight?" I blurt as Guy lets go of me.

His eyebrows jump in surprise. Did I really ask out a hottie I hardly know? I'm floored that it was so easy. But I feel like something just snapped, unshackling this fearless Amy-like side of myself I never thought existed. It's freeing.

It's exhilarating . . . until my more dominant, non-Amy side starts bracing for him to say no. I can practically already hear Guy hemming and hawing about being too busy with work or that he's dating someone. It'll be embarrassing, of course, but then I'll learn his intentions right off the bat, and I can go on with my life as if I never saw him.

Turns out I dredged up all that drama in my head for nothing, because he answers, "Yeah! Totally! I was actually gonna walk you out and suggest meeting up later after we both get some rest, but you beat me to the punch."

"Oh." The butterflies return in droves.

Guy grins again. "I guess great minds think alike."

Okay. I am fully and completely aware that anything can happen, and that I'm getting years ahead of myself, and that what I'm about to say makes me sound like Brie . . . but there's no harm in acknowledging that "Dr. Dominique Davies" has a very nice ring to it.

5

After going home and Googling Guy's name to death, I'm physically aching to call Amy and fill her in on my morning. But since it's her last full day with Joel, I decide not to disrupt them, and I go straight to bed. I'm so jumpy, though, that I keep waking up, logging zero hours of deep sleep when my alarm clock blares that afternoon.

Now running on pure adrenaline, I blaze through my daily Pilates routine before reveling in a steaming hot shower. Standing there, I try relaxing my jitters by pretending that I'm under a tropical waterfall . . . with Guy. While lathering up, I envision that his hands instead of mine are caressing every part of my body. Meanwhile, Guy's gushing about how he has waited his whole life for this, and soon I'm following him behind the waterfall to a covert rock cavern, where he has his way with me.

Following ten hot rollers, two Bioré strips, five outfit changes, and countless more pornographic fantasies starring Guy and me, I saunter into the living room at half past six.

"May I borrow the car?" I ask Dad, who's sprawled out on the couch watching the Marlins game. "I hate biking in skirts."

"You're missing dinner *again*?" He slams down his iced tea for dramatic effect and frowns disappointedly. "You know, between seeing Amy, babysitting, and candy striping, you've barely been home since you've *come* home."

"'Candy striper' is hopelessly antiquated, Dad. The proper term is 'patient care intern.'"

"Well, *excuuuuuse* me," he kids. "I had no idea higher education made you so politically correct."

"Oh, Dommie, you look lovely," Mom remarks primly from the kitchen. "Are you and Amy going out somewhere?"

"She's visiting her boyfriend, remember?"

"Oh, right." Mom shakes her head in sorrow, and I know by heart the mini-lecture she's about to deliver, having been the original inspiration for it. "I hope that girl's not getting too serious with him. College is the time to meet lots of boys. I'll never understand why children are in such a rush to act like adults."

If I thought it'd make a difference, I'd talk back, because Amy has never let her relationship stop her from meeting guys. And I truly believe being young isn't an issue as long as you're with the right person and dedicated to each other. Plus, considering we can now vote, serve on a jury, die for our country, and even get married, we technically *are* adults.

"So, if Amy's down for the count," Dad says as I begin setting the table for them, "where are you heading?"

"Big Fish."

"Why do you want to eat alone?"

"I won't be eating alone."

I think I hear the sound barrier break as my parents whip their heads around to trade puzzled expressions with each other.

"Then with *whom* will you be eating?" Mom inquires.

"Just someone I met."

"Aaaand?" they bleat.

"A third-year at Ford."

I bite my tongue to keep from laughing, and Dad sighs impatiently. "Feel free to relieve our suspense at any time. Does this mystery student have a name? A gender?"

"Yes. Both, in fact."

Dad grunts.

"Is this a *date*?" Mom asks with bated breath.

I lay out the last of the silverware. *"Maaaaybe."*

They break out into a condescending duet of *"Awws,"* and Mom says, "See? This is precisely what Amy should be doing—getting to know different people for a change. Good for you!"

"Whatever," I grumble before finally spilling the Guy details. Mom is impressed because his major involves multi-variable calculus, which is far more complex than anything she teaches in high school. But Dad, being Dad, wastes no time sizing Guy up with his signature brand of tact.

"He *isolates neutrons*? What the hell good does that do?"

"It's very sophisticated subatomic scholarship. Online I found out that Guy even won the Ford award for Excellence in Science last year. And Beta Zeta Phi has the highest average GPA of all the fraternities there."

"Big stinkin' whoop. For all we know, this *Guy* guy could be some crazy con man who prowls hospital cafeterias looking for unsuspecting candy stripers. Excuse me, *patient care interns.*"

"Ha. *So* clever. And you'll be happy to hear that I also checked him out in the metro database, and he has no criminal record, not even a traffic ticket."

"That's assuming he gave you his real name," Dad sneers. "And I suggest you go dutch tonight. If this *Guy* guy pays, he might feel entitled to pay*back,* if ya know what I mean."

"Daddy! Ew! Don't gross me out!" I make a beeline for the front door as he busts up laughing.

"Have a nice time," Mom calls after me.

"I will," I say, grabbing the keys to our station wagon from the foyer table.

Then Dad asks, "Are you coming fishing tomorrow? We'd like to spend more than three minutes with our daughter so we can really talk."

"Sure. Bye. Love you." I undo the top latch and turn the doorknob.

"We love you, too," they say in unison.

"And, Dom?" Dad adds when I'm halfway out of our apartment.

I spin around and shout back, "Yes?"

"We told you so."

I squint at them, bewildered. "Told me *what*?"

They remain silent, though the solemnity overtaking their faces is answer enough.

As much as I've been better about staying positive about everything, a part of me still doubted this day would come— not going on a date, but finding someone new whom I'd *like* to date. I know that sounds stupidly pessimistic, especially coming from a teen, though breakups are another area where youth is irrelevant. Whatever age you are when you're first burned is old enough to lose hope that you'll ever get excited about anybody else. My parents promised me I was wrong. So, yeah, they told me so.

My heart starts thumping with nerves as I ride the elevator down to the garage, and when I pull into Big Fish ten minutes later, my belly's doing full-on backflips. There's still no sign of Guy's red Accord convertible, which I caught a glimpse of this morning while we were saying goodbye in the hospital parking lot. For a moment I deliberate whether to hide out in the station wagon until I can spy him going inside first. I don't want to seem overanxious or desperate by showing up early. Then I remember that that's exactly the kind of meaningless overanalyzing that has never gotten me anywhere before. So I march through the front entrance, sit tall on a bench, and occupy myself by tooling around on my phone.

I'm checking grades again, even though I doubt the registrar's office would've released them over a holiday weekend—it didn't—when Guy strides in at seven on the dot. He's even cuter now that he's clean-shaven. In physics two years ago, we learned how gravity is the natural force of attraction between any two bodies. If I didn't know any better, I'd guess Guy's gravitational pull was reeling me in, from the way I leap to my feet and glide toward him at breakneck speed.

"Hey!" he exclaims upon seeing me. Then he puts his hand on my shoulder and gently squeezes it for a second. I think I may melt. "You look great, Dom!"

"Thanks," I reply breathily. I realize height shouldn't be important, but it's sexy that he's so much bigger than me. Even in my three-inch platform flip-flops, I only clear his collar. "So how's Bruce holding up?"

"I think his ego's hurting the worst. There're three other Betas living in the house this summer, and we're all teasing him mercilessly. How are *you*?"

"Out of it. That overnight shift threw off my whole internal clock, and I haven't eaten since I saw you."

"Me neither." He massages his temples. "And I'm feeling woozy."

"Uh-oh. Why don't we get fed before we're being raced to the ER ourselves."

"Yeah, let's do it!"

Suddenly Guy's hand flies to his mouth, and we both smile, red-faced, at each other. How bizarre that we met only this morning. It seems like much longer ago.

"What I meant was," he continues, *"so, shall we?"*

He pivots toward the hostess stand and offers me his arm, which I take, still smiling. Then something possesses me to echo his words.

"Let's do it."

6

Coincidentally, Guy received the latest *Scientific American* in the mail today. The moment we slide into our booth, he starts recapping the feature article that detailed how recent advances in quantum mechanics indicate that teleportation may be possible. Soon I'm telling him about a new book I read on the ancient Greek physician Herophilus, who went on to become the world's first anatomist. Eventually the subject turns back to Guy's summer research, and at one point he's sketching diagrams of nuclear fusion on cocktail napkins.

Anyone overhearing us would be bored to tears, but who cares? Most talking consists of banal chitchat and rumors—even the surgeons at Lee County Medical gossip in the break rooms about who's hooking up with whom—so it's refreshing to geek out on issues greater than ourselves for a change. Best of all, we never stop finding things to speak about, which was my biggest fear. Nothing's more uncomfortable than silence, unless I'm with Amy or my parents.

When Big Fish closes at eleven, I mention that we should leave an extra tip for hogging the table so long. I take out my wallet, but Guy slaps his MasterCard over the check.

"Your Cajun money's no good here, Baylor."

"Thanks, but I really want to split it."

Guy furrows his brow as I slide a twenty across the table. My reason has nothing to do with Dad's "advice." I just like things to be equal, which is how I explain it to him.

"Whatever floats your boat," he relents, "but divvying up the bill's a pain. So let me cover this, and then you can get it next time. 'Equal' enough for you?"

It's like I'm dreaming. He just disclosed that he's expecting to see me after tonight!

"Absolutely." I nod, grinning, before retrieving my cash.

"So I know this is crazy," he says a few minutes later as we descend the front steps, "but I'm hungry again."

"It's not *that* crazy. We finished our lobsters hours ago."

"I'd like to go somewhere else, but all that's still open around here is fast food. I'm getting sick of it."

"Well, you're welcome to whatever leftovers are at my place. On Saturdays my mom roasts chicken and potatoes. I think she made lemon icebox pie, too."

Instantly it hits me that asking Guy over on a first date could be construed as a green light to go a lot farther than I'm prepared to tonight. I hope he can't tell that I've already imagined us going as far as two people can. Inviting him back felt like the natural thing to offer, though, which may be a good sign in itself—I obviously trust Guy. And seeing that he's clutching his stomach, it's clear that's the only organ on his mind right now.

"Ooh. That sounds *so* good. I haven't had anything homemade in forever. And your fam would be cool with me being there?"

"Sure, not that they'll even know. They're rarely up this late."

"Sounds like a plan." He takes out his keys and starts for his Accord. "Just lead the way!"

Once inside the apartment, I show Guy to the kitchen and excuse myself to use my bathroom. There I brush my teeth, reapply deodorant, and lay out fresh hand towels in case Guy uses the bathroom at some point. Next I go out into my bedroom and get the Herophilus biography, which Guy asked to borrow. Finally I allow myself a few seconds to curl up on my carpet and giggle hysterically with elation.

Back in the kitchen, I find Guy preheating our oven.

"You can put the chicken and potatoes in the microwave, you know. It'll be quicker."

"Oh, I get it." He smiles. "You want to get rid of me sooner."

"*Nooo.*" I smile back. "I'm just trying to be helpful."

"And *I* just prefer convection to dielectric heat. It warms up food more evenly."

"Silly me. How could I have spoken such blasphemy?" I fish out two bottled waters from the fridge and hand him one. "So, were you always a physics nut?"

"More or less. The big thing that hooked me as a kid was the *Millennium Falcon* reaching light speed in *Star Wars*. I was so bummed later when I learned that could never happen under special relativity, unless Einstein's wrong."

"I've never actually watched those movies."

It's a mistake admitting that while Guy is mid-sip. He's coughing so violently, I'm afraid he'll crack a rib.

"Sorry—" He rips off a paper towel to pat his mouth. "Did I hear you right? You've never seen the original trilogy?"

"Well, I know the premise and characters and stuff, and I've caught bits and pieces on TV over the years. It seemed okay."

"Just *okay*? Now, *that's* blasphemy!" He checks the clock over the stove. "You weren't planning on going to sleep soon, were you?"

Four hours later we're on the terrace as Guy devours the last of Mom's pie, and my laptop remotely accesses his copy of *The Empire Strikes Back*. Earlier we saw *A New Hope*, and next we intend to plow through *Return of the Jedi*. We decided to watch outdoors so we could pump up the audio without disturbing my parents. Also, Guy thought it'd be cool to experience *Star Wars* actually *under* the stars.

"So what's the verdict on this one?" he asks after *Empire* ends and we both stand to stretch.

"I liked it even better than the first! It was really funny, too." I'm not exaggerating, though I'd probably enjoy any movie while six stories high against a moonlit sky and lying on adjacent lounge chairs with a hunky crush.

"Yeah. Episode five has the best laughs."

"But my favorite part was that last scene when Luke Skywalker gets the mechanical hand."

"Ha! I *knew* you would love that, biology nut."

I lean against the rail and gaze out over the city. "It's so incredible that when that was filmed, brain-controlled prosthetic limbs were pure science fiction, but now it's happening! That just makes it more infuriating, though, that a lot of the world's population still can't access even *basic* health care."

"It's the same with engineering. Inventing the technology is the easy part. Getting it to the people who need it is the real challenge."

"That's why after my residency, I'd love to do Doctors Without Borders for a while, if they accept me."

"Mmm." Guy joins me at the rail, but at the far end. "You know, Dom, a lot of the Ford premeds are in it just for money and prestige or because they're from a medical family. It's cool you're the real deal."

"Thanks. I hope that's what I am. I mean, sure, I want to help people, but that's not my only reason. Lots of professions help people somehow. It's just, nothing else ever wowed me as much as medicine, even your fancy cathode ray guns and photon emitters."

Guy grins. "It's true. The human body is eons more advanced than any machine we can build. But *I* couldn't be an MD." He turns toward me. "There's no margin for error, and I'd always be worried about messing up. It's too much pressure having that sort of responsibility for someone else. . . . Does that make me a bad person?"

"Not at all," I answer through a yawn. "My best friend,

Amy, would sooner wear a noose than a stethoscope. And you're lucky you're already in touch with what your boundaries are."

"Uh-huh. It's good to know what you want."

Without any warning, Guy whisks down the rail so he's only a couple of feet to my left and staring straight into my eyes. Now I've never felt more awake. All night I've been waiting for this moment, and I thought my having some experience would make me extra suave when the moment arrived. But in this case, experience seems to have the reverse effect, because I won't shut up as Guy continues moving toward me.

"I agree—it *is* good to know what you want. It must be frustrating majoring in one thing and then figuring out later it's all wrong for you."

Closer.

"That happened with my roommate. Starting off, she was going for a music degree, but now she's doubling in communications and women's studies!"

Leaning in.

"At Tulane, something like one out of every three premeds ends up switching—"

Guy slips his hand to the nape of my neck, bends down, and kisses me lightly on the mouth. I pucker back, though my blood is pounding so ferociously that I hardly feel him, and it takes all my mental energy to keep my knees from buckling.

Afterward he tilts his head forward, leaving us in a suspended Eskimo kiss. I'd forgotten how surreal being this close to someone is—as if the rest of the planet has fallen away, leaving just us two to do just this.

"It's funny," he begins, his lemony breath hot on my face. "I was so pissed at Bruce for making me spend the night in the hospital. Now I owe the dude."

I'm too exultant to respond, not that I'd know what to say to that, so I just manage a little nod. Soon he pulls back and retreats to his lounge chair.

"Sorry, Dom. I wasn't planning on doing that here. You're just so freakin' pretty, and under the moon, your hair's, like, on fire."

"Oh— No— It's— I'm— Don't worry about it."

"We'd better stop, though. I feel nervous mackin' on you with your parents inside. I don't want to risk them catching us."

I nod again and make myself pause for a deep breath. "Yeah. That's probably a wise idea." I wobble over to my chair.

I try to get into *Jedi,* but my vision is foggy from the enormity of what just happened. My biggest "step forward" to date. Proof that I really am "moving on to bigger and better things." The first kiss of the rest of my life. *I can't believe I've kissed someone else!* It felt similar and completely different at the same time, kind of like mounting a new bike— same basic stance, but still unfamiliar. I'm so glad that it was with Guy and not some anonymous boy at a kegger, and that I'm not some anonymous girl to him. The kiss wouldn't have been nearly as special. . . .

The next thing I'm conscious of is Mom's voice telling me to wake up. Now her hand is shaking my shoulder, and I can sense that it's light out. Evidently, pulling two all-nighters in a row was too ambitious for me.

"Dommie, are you all right? Why are you out here?"

I slit open my eyelids, which feel as heavy as lead as I scan the terrace. Guy's chair is empty. The sun is just starting to peek up over the skyline. My laptop is still on our small patio table, but the screen is down.

"How was Big Fish? Did you have fun?" Mom persists, looking hilarious in her muumuu and bunny slippers.

"Uh . . . hold on a sec."

Intuitively I lift up the computer screen, and a Word document appears.

Good Morning, Sleeping Beauty–
You nodded off when the Ewoks showed up. Can't say I blame you. A lot of people think they're the worst part of the series. I don't have the heart to wake you, so I'll take that book you lent me and let myself out. Had a great time, and tell your fam I said thanks for the eats. Today I'm just gonna catch up on Z's and work, but I'll call later to see when you'll be up for round two. ;)
–Guy

My heart skipping a beat, I click to see when the file was created. 5:10 a.m. Guy and I spent nearly half a day together.

"When did you get back? What were you doing?" Mom is still rambling. *What happened to all the food?*

They're perfectly legitimate questions deserving of explanations, but I don't have the patience right now. I was also in the middle of a raunchy dream about Guy as Han Solo and me as Princess Leia in our own private starship, and I want to get back to bed in the hopes of resuming it.

I mutter to Mom, "Guy came over. We watched movies.

Finished the leftovers. He says thanks. I need sleep," before grabbing the laptop and hurtling toward my room.

I feel guilty. There's no way I'll have the energy to go fishing with my parents today, and I already sacrificed last Sunday's outing by sleeping in at Amy's. But I wouldn't trade my Guy time for anything, and I console myself with the knowledge that there're still six more Sundays of summer vacation left.

I remain zonked out through the afternoon, and when I wake up, I burst into laughter again. How glorious that what began as my worst Fourth of July weekend ever transformed into my best! I take advantage of having the apartment to myself by blasting CeCe Peniston's "Finally" on repeat while I do laundry, exercise, and indulge in a bubble bath that could only be better with Guy in it.

My parents return right as Amy texts me that her stepdad just brought her home from the airport. Three minutes later, I'm pedaling to the Braffs'.

7

Amy's response is as I expected—high-pitched squeals and a "Hallelujah" before dashing to where I'm perched on her Papasan chair for a hug.

"I knew the second I saw your glow, Dom, that something major must've gone down this weekend! Happy Independence Day to *you*!" Now dancing in place, she begins belting out *Grease* lyrics: *"Summer lovin', had me a blast! Summer lovin', happened so fast!"*

"Let's not jinx it," I say, smiling at her enthusiasm. "It was only a first date."

Amy then demands "a visual." Guy has already friended me on Facebook, so I pull up his profile photo on my phone.

"Holy hotness! Break me off a piece of that!" She keeps dancing. *"Tell me more, tell me more. Did you get very far?"*

"I told you, just one closed-mouth kiss. *And, like, he does have a car.*"

"Did he get hard?"

"Oh, good lord." I crack up. As juvenile as we sound, sometimes the most fun thing in the world is laughing with girls about boys. "I doubt it. We were lip to lip for only a moment."

"Well, it's just fabulous that at long last this is all happening! I really thought you were too scared—" She stops short. "Strike that. Brain fart."

"Yeah, right. What's there to be scared of?"

"You know . . ." She shrugs uncomfortably. "Maybe getting hurt again like you were by a certain former track teammate of mine. For a while there, you were sure you wouldn't *ever* feel better."

After a protracted breath I shake my head. "Actually, I've never been scared. I don't think I *could* get hurt again, at least not as badly. I'm, like, inoculated now."

"Not necessarily. My mom has counseled people on their second or third major split, and sometimes those breakups are way tougher than the first."

"Yay. Something to look forward to." I lean back and stare at the ceiling. "I wonder if it *would* be possible to create a heartbreak vaccine. I'd win the Nobel Prize."

"Sorry, Dom. I didn't mean to bring up sad stuff. And I'm really sorry about Brie-*dzilla* at the barbecue. Ever since Matt got down on one knee, she has acted like an authority on everyone else's private life. She'll say crap to me like, 'You and Joel are next!' And I'm like, *'I'm barely nineteen!*

Get a clue!' Besides, after this weekend, I'm wondering if it wouldn't be better if Joel and I just called it quits."

"Oh, no!" I sit up again, astounded that even Amy can sound so cavalier about this. "What happened with you guys?"

"Nothing bad, but nothing amazing, either. If only he and I could rewind to *our* first date. Things were so much more exciting before we saw each other burp, or with boogers, and we didn't know each other's faults yet. Now all the mystery is gone. In Kansas, I was hoping that a few romps in the great outdoors would spice things up with us, but can I just say, campsite coitus is almost more trouble than it's worth." She lifts up the hem of her blouse to reveal dozens of fresh chigger bites on her back.

"Ick. You're gonna be itching for days."

"And on the flight here, I got so mad at myself for leaving home just because of a guy. How did *I* become the type who travels fifteen hundred miles for eight inches?"

I roll my eyes. "Because Joel isn't just any 'guy.' And you've been together since August. And you have a ton in common. And you're in love with each other . . . unless you've changed your stance on him?"

"No," she says flatly before fetching calamine lotion from the bathroom. "I don't mean to whine so much. I get that these are 'good problems' to have. It's just this long-distance thing makes everything harder, but I'm preaching to the choir on that one."

"Yeah, but distance wasn't all bad. When Tulane started, it was nice being able to focus on school without having a boyfriend right there. I don't know how I would've found enough time to study otherwise."

"Well, I'm definitely getting a lot done without Joel around. I'm keeping up my running and sketching, and I'm already looking into gallery jobs for next year."

"See? And if you two can get through this summer, then you can probably get through anything. Being separated is like a litmus test for a relationship, so think of it as an experiment."

"Huh . . . maybe," she says, more upbeat. "Which reminds me. I take it recent developments have put the kibosh on *your* 'experiment'?"

I'm about to ask what she means, when the answer erupts in my head, and I feel my stomach knot. After a pause I admit, "Haven't thought about it. Ever since the hospital yesterday, Cal kinda dropped off my radar."

"That seems pretty conclusive to me, *Coppertone*."

"Ugh. If things progress with Guy, I guess I'll have to tell Cal. Friends tell friends when they're dating someone, right?"

"Prepare yourself, because that conversation's gonna suck! He'll act happy for you, but you know it'll ruin all his hopes and crush his little lovelorn heart."

"Please, Ames. Don't feel the need to sugarcoat the situation," I quip sarcastically. "It's not like Cal's feelings are monumentally important to me or anything."

But by nightfall, Calvin is pushed out of my mind again when Guy follows through on his word to call and reiterates that last night/this morning rocked. We then compare schedules, only to discover that we won't be able to see each other again until the weekend—that's five more days. I consider canceling one of my bratsitting gigs to make time for him sooner. But even if I didn't need the spending money, I don't want to fall back into old patterns of letting a boy consume my life. Besides, I'm thrilled just to have someone like Guy to miss.

Guy calls on Monday, Tuesday, and Wednesday, which to me is as good as kisses. Any sign that I'm being thought about by a boy *I'm* thinking about is all I need to feel secure in his feelings for me. So when I don't hear from Guy on Thursday, rationally I know that nothing has changed and he probably still likes me . . . but emotions aren't rational. And since I refuse to agonize over a boy ever again if I can help it, I decide to take control and phone him for reassurance. Who says that initiating communication is a dating rule "don't"?

"Hey, Dom," he answers brightly. "What's happening?"

"Not much. I'm about to go to bed, and I felt like saying hey." After all, I shouldn't need any better excuse to contact someone who's on track to be my boyfriend.

"It's that late already? Damn, I haven't even left lab yet. Sometimes time gets away from me when I'm in the flow."

"Oh, I didn't know you were working now. I'll let you get back to it—"

"Not so fast. You still free to hang out tomorrow after the hospital?"

"Yeah, of course!" I exclaim, half-jubilant that all seems well with us, and half-angry at myself for worrying that it wasn't. I wish my imagination weren't so prone to run wild with worst-case scenarios.

"Cool. If you don't mind trekking to my 'hood, I can show you what I do all day."

"That'd be great! I haven't been to Ford in forever."

We then plan for me to park my bike at his place so we can walk to the Physical Sciences Complex together.

"Beta's the big green house at the end of Fraternity Row," he tells me.

"Got it. So, I guess I'll see you soon, then."

"Not soon enough, but oh, well. Till tomorrow."

My breath shudders, and I can't help but project way into the future. It'd be so cute if we sent out engagement announcement cards with the heading "the physicist and the physician."

"Till tomorrow, Guy."

8

The following evening, Guy answers the Beta house door with a smile and a kiss, before taking me, as planned, to his lab. While he proceeds to demonstrate how all the equipment operates with the same zeal as a kid in a toy store, I'm reminded of my only teacher crush, Mr. Chesnoff from tenth-grade chemistry. It was never my favorite science subject, but he was so brilliant and passionate in that sexy professor kind of way that I attended all his extra-help sessions just so I could have an excuse to stare at him.

An hour later, as we're exiting the Physical Sciences Complex, Guy proposes having dinner at a nearby sushi bar that gives student discounts on Fridays. "One of the Betas is studying abroad in Tokyo and keeps blogging about the food, so now I'm jonesing for it."

"Sounds good, but you'll have to help me order. I've never had sushi before."

Immediately, Guy stops and gazes off into the distance.

"You okay?" I ask.

"Yeah. I'm just trying to decide which is more tragic—life without *Star Wars* or life without spicy tuna hand rolls. . . . I think it's a toss-up."

"Hey, buddy! I've been managing just fine without either."

"No matter. My mission is clear. Somebody has to introduce you to the finer things." Then he slings his arm over my shoulder and leads me to the restaurant.

By nightfall, Guy and I have put away an entire sampler platter. I was afraid sushi would be slimy, but it's lighter and tastier than it looks. My impression may have more to do with the setting, though, which includes a corner table, dark lighting, and bluesy jazz playing in the background with a very suggestive bass beat. Guy even insists on paying again in return for cleaning out my parents' fridge last time. Then afterward, as we're strolling back to campus, he winds his arm around my waist. It seems like forever since I've been this happy, which is a whole different ball game than feeling content or satisfied or blessed. I'm so happy, I don't care how sad it is that I needed a boy to reach this level.

"So, wanna hang out inside?" Guy asks as we approach my bike. "You already showed me your pad. It's only 'equal' that I show you mine."

I knew this was coming, but my pulse springs up to three digits anyway. Before I can say anything, he adds, "Wait. Let me guess. You've never been to a frat house before, either."

I cock my head at him. "I'm not *that* sheltered. For Saint Patrick's, some girlfriends and I went to a Sigma Nu bash. Although, we never did get past the yard—it was too packed."

"Well, crowds won't be a problem tonight. Everyone's at a bar crawl, so we'll have the place to ourselves." He shoots me a sultry grin, and it's good that it's dark out so he can't see my cheeks burn at what we both know he's suggesting.

"The thing is, if I stay, it can't be for more than an hour or two." I inform him how Amy's leaving early tomorrow for her bridesmaid-dress fitting in Tampa, and I already promised to spend the day with her and take turns driving there. "I need a full night's sleep so I'm not bushed for the trip."

"That's cool. We'll make the most of our time." He grins again before charging up the front steps.

Beta's ground level is laid out like a typical home, except it has a ton more couches and the biggest wide-screen I've ever seen. Crumbs and dust bunnies coat every flat surface. A three-foot stack of porno DVDs is piled right next to the Wii games. And no matter where you turn, there's a wasteland of alcohol paraphernalia—discarded beer bottle caps, dirty shot glasses, a funnel tube. . . . The second level resembles a traditional boys' dorm, complete with a long central hallway and the omnipresent odor of Febrezed-over pee. So all in all, it's tamer than I envisioned. As Guy keys his lock, my heart speeds up again. Although I'm glad his brothers aren't around to sidetrack him, being alone intensifies the atmosphere even more.

Guy flips on his bed lamp, revealing his room to be surprisingly bare. It needs vacuuming like the rest of the house, and the trash can's overflowing with empty chip bags and take-out boxes. Otherwise, there's little else besides a lava lamp by the window, a barbell in the corner, a bobble head on his dresser, and a triple-screen monitor on his desk.

"Wow, I never pegged you as a hoarder," I joke.

Guy smiles. "I try never to have more stuff than I can fit in my car. I hate feeling weighed down."

"That's smart." I recall the six giant suitcases required to pack up my dorm room, and that's not counting all the boxes I put in storage.

Next I take a closer look at the bobble head, which is a man wearing a colonial-looking coat and holding an apple. On the base it says SIR ISAAC NEWTON (1642–1727).

"So is he, like, your idol?" I ask.

"Let's just say I'd give up sushi for good if I could be as badass as him."

"Yeah, I guess it *is* pretty huge figuring out gravity."

"*And* calculus. *And* optics. *And* the laws of motion. And what's insane is, he came up with a lot of that stuff in the two years Cambridge closed down during the bubonic plague. So he essentially founded modern science *on vacation!*"

I shake my head. "I'm so jealous. That kind of genius is unreal."

"Yeah, but brains are worth crap unless you put in the time. Newton was such a workaholic, he died a virgin."

I laugh nervously. That was the *last* thing I expected to hear. "Like . . . that's documented fact?"

"It's pretty much assumed. There're hilarious stories of

John Locke bringing him women and Newton getting mad and turning them away."

I laugh again. "I guess that explains where he got all his time to innovate."

I scan the room for a less sexual conversation topic. Then I notice that the bed opposite Guy's is stripped. "I thought Bruce roomed here also."

"He does, during the year. But there're few enough residents now that we don't have to share digs. He's across the hall for the summer."

Suddenly Guy shuts the door behind us. My heart spasms in anticipation. I take a seat on the bare mattress and keep the dialogue going.

"So, is Bruce researching in your lab, too?"

"Nah-uh. He's working at the campus observatory through July, and then at the planetarium next month."

Guy sits on his own bed.

"Were you friends before pledging Beta?"

"No. We had the same intro classes, since he's majoring in astronomy, but I didn't really get to know him till Hell Week."

Guy slides off his watch.

"'Hell Week'? Uh-oh. So you were hazed?"

"Oh, yeah. The suckiest was the night Bruce and I were woken up at three a.m. and locked in a closet together with a raw onion. They wouldn't let us out until it was gone."

Guy unlaces his sneakers.

"You *ate* a whole raw onion? *Sooooo* nasty."

"P.S. Afterward we had to smoke a cigar, and then we weren't allowed to brush our teeth for two days."

Guy slips off his shoes.

"I'm sorry. That's plain abusive."

"But effective. Nothing bonds people more than going through shit together."

Guy pulls off his polo, exposing a tight, white Hanes T-shirt.

"Still, stories like that are what made me too scared to rush at Tulane."

"It's worth it in the end, though. I'm alone in the lab so much, I like coming home to an actual house where there's always people over and stuff happening. Well, that's not the case now, obviously. Campus is dead in the summer."

Guy empties his pockets of his phone, Altoids, and wallet, which falls open as he sets it on the floor. I see that one of the credit card slots contains a condom.

"But it must be nice having a room to yourself. That's such a luxury in college."

"Yeah, it's, uh . . . it's definitely convenient."

Guy scoots back on the bed and lies on his side so he's against the wall and his head is propped up on his bent arm. He's giving me that hungry look like he did on my terrace.

"So, Dom, I know there's not much space here, but"—he places his other hand flat in front of him and pats the sheets—"care to join?"

I didn't know it was possible to feel this ecstatic, wary, and turned on all at the same time. After a deep breath, I stand up and tentatively cross the two yards of space separating us. Instead of lying next to him, though, I kneel by the bed and place my hand on his.

So, *of course* I want to hook up with Guy. If you haven't

already picked up on it, that has pretty much become my default daydream. But I love where he and I stand right now. It's like we're on the brink, and everything's full of excitement and potential precisely because the heavy making out is still something to look forward to. I realize we can't remain PG-rated forever. I'm all too aware, though, how easy it is to let hooking up become the crux of a relationship. Then you forget how to just *be* together and why you should *stay* together. So for the meantime I'd like to take things slowly in order to prevent hooking up from ever getting too important.

Amy would say I'm overreacting, but I'm just trying to learn from past mistakes. And if Guy isn't an asshole, which I'm confident he's not, he'll go along with it.

I'm about to speak, but Guy pipes up first. "This might sound strange, but you smell really good."

Even stranger than his saying that is that I'm thinking the same thing about him. It's not of anything in particular. His aftershave has long since worn off. He just smells . . . right.

Abruptly, Guy sits up, cups my face in his hands, and gives me a long, soft kiss. Then a harder one so my lips are smashed against my teeth. Next he slides his mouth down to my neck, and I giggle when his poufy hair tickles my cheeks and chin. Soon we're kissing again as his hands run up and down my sides, and it feels so amazing—like little fireworks beneath the surface—that I wonder how I've been able to live for the last several months without being touched like this. It's a medical fact that babies are less likely to survive if they're not frequently held, so has my skin been starving all this time? Within the minute, though, Guy begins pulling me toward him onto the bed, and I sense the tip of his tongue pressing between my lips. I jerk back.

"Oh, crap," he says, holding his hand over his mouth. "Does my breath reek of soy sauce? I took two Altoids."

"Oh, no. You're fine. It's, um . . . it's me."

"You need time to digest or something?"

I laugh again. "No. It's, uh . . ."

I stand and pace and strain to come up with the words while each of my body's fifty trillion cells is screaming for me to rip the Hanes off this younger and cuter Mr. Chesnoff type, who's mine for the taking.

"It's just that . . . I would like . . . to wait more . . . before we go . . . any further."

"Oh." He doesn't look angry. Just confused. "All right."

I raise my eyebrow at him. "You sure that's okay?"

"Yeah . . . Well, it's not what I'd *choose,* but, Dom . . ." He sits up and gazes plaintively at me. "I'm really sorry. I hope you didn't feel, you know, pressured or anything. I swear I thought you wanted to mess around."

"I did! I do!" I kneel down again so we're eye level. "Everything that has happened so far has been great. And it's not that I haven't done any of this before. I've done *a lot* more. But for now I just . . . I want . . . For me . . . It's hard to explain."

"You don't have to." He holds up his hands in surrender. "You're just not ready or whatever."

Actually, the more accurate assessment is that *we're* not ready, but there's no point in splitting hairs when he's taking this as well as I could've hoped. He seems uneasy, though, so

I sidle next to him and say, "Guy, I've loved every minute of tonight. I don't want you to think anything's spoiled."

"Hell, no! Dom, you're the first girl I've met this summer who I look forward to just talking to." He wraps his hands around the top of my head. "I like what's in *here*." He squeezes. "As for everything else, *you* set the pace."

My eyes start tearing. "Thanks, Guy, for being so cool. Lots of boys wouldn't be."

"I've never understood that—that there're some dudes who'd make a girl feel bad for not putting out. How could a guy enjoy it if the girl doesn't really want it?"

"I don't know, but it's sad so many girls think they're undatable if they don't go all the way. I'd *never* do it just to please a boy," I say proudly. However, I immediately question whether that's totally accurate. Although it was my idea to start having sex back when I did, at least a tiny part of my motivation may have been to try to receive extra commitment in return. I hoped that having sex would add formality and legitimacy to being in a relationship, and that it would elevate us to a higher plane than merely two star-crossed teenagers in love.

"Anyway," Guy goes on, "I'm just glad you spoke up before. And *please* keep telling me what's on your mind, because apparently I suck at reading it. I don't want to do *anything* with you unless you're on board." He casts down his eyes. "I'd feel so guilty if you ever regretted something we did."

"Aw, I never doubted that." I wrap my arms around him and lean against his shoulder. That he's sensitive to this stuff makes him all the more attractive.

"Damn," Guy says. "Nothing like a little wellness seminar on a Friday night, huh?"

I laugh. "Still, it feels really nice being so open about everything."

"Yeah." He throws his arms around me too. "It does."

We continue holding each other as we share a long silence. There's no awkwardness, though. I'm more comfortable with him than ever. Eventually Guy asks, "How about we go downstairs and finish watching episode six till you have to leave?"

I plant a kiss on his cheek, grab his hand, and pull him off the bed. *"Let's do it."*

9

"Sushi?" Dad repeats disgustedly while stringing his fishing rod. It's eleven a.m. on Sunday, and my parents and I are finally together on our little boat, drifting along Pine Island Sound. " 'Sushi' is just a fancy word for 'bait.' "

"Millions of people eat it every day, Dad. Raw seafood is a delicacy."

"Delicacy, shmelicacy. If I took one of the seven-pounders I intend to reel in today and bit off its flesh with my bare teeth, that wouldn't be so delicate, would it? The mark of civilized man is using fire to cook his kills!"

"Whatever." I finish applying sunblock to my face. "Guy and I had fun."

"Are you sure you want to keep seeing him?" Mom prods.

I look at her like she's crazy. "Um, *yeah*. Why shouldn't I?"

I'm sorry for asking. Mom takes it as another cue to harp on how this isn't the time to be tying myself down to one person. So I just tune her out while concentrating on what a wonderful weekend it's been so far.

After *Jedi* on Friday, Guy walked me to my bike, where he kissed me goodnight and promised to call the following evening. Then in Tampa yesterday, Amy and I laughed our way through Bonnie's Bridesmaids Salon, the Lowry Park Zoo, and the museum of art, not to mention the two-hour-plus car ride each way. When I got in last night, Guy phoned like he said he would, told me about an NPR story he just heard on stem cells, and asked when he could see me again. So now I'm counting the hours—seven—until he picks me up this evening. At the dentist's last week I read an article in *Cosmo* claiming that couples can't say they're officially together until they've gone out three times. It's a groundless rule, though I'm still giddy about tonight being *our* third date.

". . . but despite all that," Mom concludes, "your father and I are glad you're getting out there and having a good time. And we're very impressed at how well you've been balancing that with your work responsibilities."

"Even if it means *we* haven't seen you for so much as a meal," Dad ribs.

"Sorry, guys. I'll try to be better. And I'm here now!"

"Indeed you are," Mom says provocatively. "And while we finally have you to ourselves for a while, we'd like to share some important news."

I look up from my tackle box, suddenly not feeling so well. My parents *never* have news, important or not. The only "new" thing that has happened is that Dad's now sporting a fully shaved head, an act of defiance after begrudgingly accepting that the toupee he bought last month didn't fool anybody.

My face turns to stone. "Is one of you sick?"

"No, God forbid!" Dad exclaims, setting down his rod. "Your mom and I are just going to be . . . making a change."

"Change" is as bad as "news," and next I think of divorce. This year the parents of two of my dorm-mates separated. One of the girls said it was because of empty-nest syndrome, and the other girl said her parents had planned to split for years but held out until she started Tulane so she wouldn't have to live through the upheaval. But my parents don't have a hint of dysfunction in them. They're a sickeningly cute couple whose biggest fights revolve around how best to cook the fish they catch. Furthermore, Mom's schoolhouse decorum is a perfect counterbalance to Dad's jailhouse gruffness, so I don't know how either could hope to find a more compatible match. Plus they're grinning, which you don't typically do before announcing the breakup of a marriage.

"Now," Mom begins, "we know this is unexpected, but—"

"You're pregnant?" I scream.

"Dommie, please . . ."

I don't hear her over the pounding in my ears. I just recall Amy teasing me about how after I went to college my parents would rejuvenate their sex lives by getting it on all over the apartment since they wouldn't have to worry about me walking in on them.

"Oh, God!" I wail, envisioning their fleshy bellies jiggling while they do it against the kitchen counter, without protection, no less. "You know, when I was little I used to *beg* for a brother or sister, and *now,* when I don't even *live* here anymore, you—"

"Get a grip!" Dad yells. "We are *not* expecting a baby."

My heart's still lurching. "You sure, Mom?"

"Of course! Nor do we desire another child."

"You're handful enough." Dad crosses his arms at me.

"So"—I catch my breath—"just tell me!"

"We're relocating!" Mom chirps.

Dad then reveals that a big-time law enforcement consulting firm in Gainesville phoned three weeks ago to offer him a higher-paying job. "Your mom and I can't wait to take this boat out lake fishing there—"

"Wait . . . We're *moving*? And you've known about this since *June*?"

"You were still studying for exams when Daddy got the call, so we thought it best not to distract you."

"Anyhow, your mom and I needed time to consider this on our own. We only just decided—"

"But what about *your* job, Mom?"

"Well, I spoke with the school board last week, and we agreed that I'll stay on until winter break. In the meantime, they'll search for a replacement to take over after the holidays."

Dizzy with disbelief that my old headmaster knew we were moving before I did, I lean back against the side of the boat so I won't keel over. "But everything's fine in Fort Myers. Things have been fine here for two decades!"

"We're looking toward the *next* two decades," Dad states. "I'm antsy for a new challenge, and at this point in my life I'd like a quieter desk gig. But I'm just happy that, with the extra money, your mom can finally take some time off and get that master's."

I didn't even know she wanted one. She might have mentioned it before, but just in passing.

"You know, Dommie, listening to you talk about Tulane all year made me so nostalgic for university life," Mom says whimsically. "And UF has a graduate program in mathematics!"

"What if you don't get in?"

"Dom!" Dad reproaches, but Mom doesn't seem bothered.

"Then I'll keep reapplying and tutor in the interim like I've been doing during the summers. And there're always online degrees. But just think, maybe this time next year we'll *both* be students!"

She smiles at me, her emerald eyes sparkling in the sunlight, but I turn away and look out over the water.

"Aw, honey," she goes on. "I understand your being surprised, but not upset. Remember, *you* applied to UF for your safety school, and you liked the city well enough when we all toured it for you. Gainesville is still Florida. Only more inland."

"I just don't see how you guys could make a choice this ginormous without at least consulting me first."

"Well, would you really have told us to pass up this opportunity?" Mom asks.

I . . . suppose not. But still.

She continues, "And it's not as if this will impact your

72

daily life in the slightest. You just said you no longer live here."

"This all makes me feel really unimportant, though."

"That's a load of crap," Dad says sharply. "We've always put you first. Remember years back when the governor asked me to replace that Palm Beach sheriff who resigned? It would've been a great opportunity and a lot more dough, but we said no 'cause we didn't want to uproot *you*. But you're settled at college now, so it's time to do what's good for *us*. We've thought long and hard, and we promise this is a smart step."

"So when's this *relocation* going to happen?" I growl.

Dad explains that the firm wants him to start the first of the year, so tomorrow he's meeting with a real estate agent to discuss selling our apartment and finding a new place in Alachua County.

"Which means," Mom breaks in, "that you should start packing up your room before you leave for school next month. We're hoping to move the bulk of our things over Thanksgiving so we can leave town immediately after my last day of work in December."

This may be the first time I've ever felt seasick.

"Please," Mom pleads, "don't be gloomy. Life is about adapting and moving on. This is a new chapter in our lives, and we're so excited about what's next. Be happy for us."

How can I be happy about transferring my home base to a city where I have zero ties and that's 250 miles away from Guy? And how can anyplace be home without Amy?

Like a brat, I ignore my parents for the remainder of the boat trip. It sucks because, up until Mom and Dad dropped

the bomb, today was like old times, and aside from their pe-
riodic preachiness, I honestly don't mind being with them.
But now it's all I can do not to jump overboard so I won't
have to hear them babble about how they'll be buying all
new freshwater fishing equipment.

Coming home afterward just makes me more nauseated,
because, for the first time in my life, I know it's only temporary. I escape to my soon-to-be-ex-bedroom and freak
out over the phone to Amy, who promises I'll always have
a place to stay at the Braffs' house. She then points out that
if Guy goes home to Atlanta for winter break and I go to
Gainesville, he will actually have an easier time driving to
visit me, since Atlanta is a lot closer to Gainesville than it is
to Fort Myers. And considering Guy's already a junior, he'll
probably leave Fort Myers himself in two years.

By that evening I'm still stupefied and fuming and
dreading the thought of moving, but I keep telling myself
to be grateful that at least the news wasn't something truly
catastrophic.

"Hey, guys," I say awkwardly when I skulk into the living room.

Dad's watching the Marlins game while Mom's in the
kitchen sharpening her filet knife. They look at me expec-
tantly, so I take a deep breath and say what I ought to have
said back on the boat.

"Dad . . . congratulations on the job. You should be
really proud."

He exhales and nods. "Thanks, Dom."

"And, Mom . . . going back to school . . . that's really
cool. I can help with your application if you'd like."

Mom nods, too. "I'd appreciate that. You're certainly the

expert in the family, and it's been quite a while since I composed a résumé."

"So, I take it you're eating out again." Dad motions to my purse.

"Yeah. Guy just texted that he's on his way. . . . I'm sure he'll come up if you want to meet him."

I'm shocked that I suggested that after only two dates, especially when meeting the parents is a potential land mine of humiliations. Maybe I'm just anxious to remind Mom and Dad that they're not the only ones moving forward with their lives.

"Oh, no, Dommie—we can't possibly have company now!" Mom frantically shakes her latex-gloved hands. "I'm still windblown and smell of fish!"

"But if you two come here later to watch more movies, we'll have plenty of fresh snapper in the fridge for you to get your sushi fix," Dad says with a joking smile.

"Thanks," I reply, still too ticked about everything to smile back. "Well, I'd better go down, but I'll be home for dinner tomorrow. I promise."

As I wait in front of the building, I wonder whether I should've postponed seeing Guy to another night when I'm in a better frame of mind. I'd hate to be a sourpuss in front of him and risk turning him off. On the other hand, I shouldn't have to hide my moods with a potential significant other. When a boy likes you, he likes you even when you're sad.

It ends up being a moot point, though. There's something about the sight of a gorgeous guy in an open convertible heading in your direction that makes all bad feelings evaporate into thin air.

10

I tell Guy about the move first thing, and he agrees that my parents shouldn't have kept me in the dark this long. But he also agrees with what Mom said about how it won't affect my daily life, which for some reason resonates a lot more coming from him. Then, by the time we finish our crab leg dinner, two rounds of mini-golf, and an IMAX on Antarctica while Guy rests his hand on my knee, I'm too blissful to mope about Gainesville at all.

After the movie, we're strolling down Bantam Beach when we come across a recessed patch of shoreline hidden by a sand cliff. It's just beckoning for us to steal away there. I figure Guy and I have done enough non-intimate, relationship-building activities for one evening, so I stop short and look in all directions by the light of the full moon to confirm that nobody else is here. And since I know through Dad that the FMPD doesn't patrol this area at night, there's no risk of an awkward run-in with cops recognizing me as the police chief's daughter. Finally, I walk into the sandy alcove, recline on the ground, and grin up at Guy. Without a word, he grins back and lies down next to me.

I never would have thought that fooling around without rounding any "bases" could be so erotic. The scalp massage Guy gives me feels a lot nicer than sex ever did, and it definitely lasts longer and isn't as messy. Withholding also forces us to be creative, like when Guy makes up a game where he draws letters on my back with his fingers for me to decipher. As if the sensation of his thumb skating up and around my spine doesn't make me tingly enough, he spells out the most flattering words: "beautiful," "amazing," "brainiac." But the best is when I start rubbing Guy's shoulders, which he complains have been achy from hunching over his lab table, and he groans with pleasure. "This is just what I needed, Dom. I could stay like this all summer. I'm so happy right now."

I have to bite my tongue so I don't howl for joy. *I* am the catalyst for Guy Davies being "so happy"! I doubt that getting straight As in my summer electives could make me feel any more triumphant.

When I'm done with his shoulders, we resurvey the surroundings to be sure we're still alone, before falling back to the ground and reverting to straight kissing. But I guess you can skirt the baselines for only so long.

"Oh. Sorry," Guy says after his hand grazes my boob. "I didn't mean—"

"I know. It's okay." I resume nuzzling his neck.

"Actually, we should quit now. I'm getting too worked up if this is as far as it's going."

"Oh . . . all right." I sit up and shake the sand out of my hair.

"But one thing first." He grabs me by the waist and gives me a lingering kiss.

"Mmm," I hum when he pulls back. "That should hold me till next time."

"I wish *I* could hold you till next time."

It's a good thing I'm not standing, because this is the closest I've ever felt to swooning.

"Quick," he commands while lying back and squeezing his eyes shut. "Let's talk about something, anything. Keep my mouth moving so I won't attack you with it."

"Okay. Um . . ." I wasn't going to bring this up yet, but it seems needless now to wait any longer. "I know this is, like, over a month in advance, but that wedding for Amy's stepbrother is on August sixteenth. It's supposed to be really nice, and I was invited with a guest. So if you're okay with spending a Saturday night in a suit, would you be my 'plus one'?"

"Count me in," he replies right away.

I feel so grown-up all of a sudden. A college under-classman being escorted by a college upperclassman to an actual wedding. High school dances seem like child's play by comparison. I grin, thinking back to when I was eleven and first saw Matt at Amy's house. I thought he was the handsomest boy ever, and, having no better male outlet at school, I *like* liked him for the next several years. Of course he didn't know I was alive, and I was so envious when Brie came on the scene. How cool that now I'll be witnessing their nuptials with someone I *like* like way better.

Soon Guy and I are retracing our steps down the shore as I give him the 411 on Matt and Brie. He interrupts me when I mention that they graduated two months ago.

"Huh, so they're not much older than us. I hope they have a prenup."

"Guy!" I pinch his side and laugh. "You haven't even met them yet, and you're as bad as Amy."

"Just being realistic. I also took sociology for a distribution requirement, and the studies are clear: The younger you commit, the more likely you'll split."

"Cute rhyme, but you can't control when you meet the right person. Matt and Brie have stuck it out since they were sixteen, so something's clicking." I'm shocked that I just defended Brie.

Guy yawns. "But how can they be sure they're right for each other if they've never had anyone else to check them against?"

That's something my mom would say, and for a moment I'm paranoid she's been secretly coaching him. Then again, she and Dad were barely twenty-four when they met and married, which by Guy's standards would be really young also.

"So, you think Matt and Brie should just date other people for a while?"

"I dunno. Probability-wise it would boost their chances."

He yawns again. "And this is all assuming that getting hitched is even a feasible idea. It's a primeval institution."

Flinching, I look over at Guy's face. He appears unaware of the cognitive dissonance of saying that to someone he just said he was "so happy" with.

"But, Guy, marriage is nothing like it used to be. It's no longer about dowries and controlling women. Now it's a fifty-fifty partnership based on love."

"Yeah, but in class we talked about how we're living longer, thanks to medicine." He winks at me. "So now more spouses are growing apart before one of them can die."

"Well, the whole challenge of tying the knot is to try to *grow together.*"

"I guess, but that's kinda unnatural. And in the end, there're never any guarantees it'll work out. Half the time it doesn't."

I'm silent for a few steps. "So . . . I take it your parents are divorced?"

He laughs. "No, but they should be. I vaguely remember them being fun when I was little, but now they sleepwalk through the day with nothing interesting to say to each other."

"Maybe that's just how they operate, though."

"I don't know. I once overheard my mom tell my aunt that she'd think about leaving if she wasn't worried about supporting herself."

"Oh. Sorry. That sucks . . . but it doesn't always turn out like that. *My* parents are still going strong."

"Glad to hear it," he responds absently before changing subjects to an academic paper he wrote on entropy that he's trying to get published in some scholarly journal, not that I'm listening.

In retrospect, it makes sense that Guy is skeptical about marriage. He said his reason for not becoming a doctor is that he doesn't want responsibility for someone else. He explained that he doesn't have lots of stuff so he'll never feel weighed down. And he's right that odds are against young couples lasting—I'm walking proof of that. But that doesn't mean that they *can't* last. For it to happen, though, both people in the relationship need to *want* it to last, against all odds.

"You okay?" Guy asks. "'Cause you don't look it."

"I've got a headache," I say, which is the truth.

"Care for another scalp massage?" He starts kneading my crown with his fingers, but I instinctively crane my neck away. Then he says, "I'll help distract you from the pain." He leans over and nibbles my earlobe, spurring me to throw his arm off my shoulder and sprint away from him up the beach.

"Yikes, Dom. You really don't feel well."

"I'll be okay. Just give me a minute."

He comes up behind me. "What can I do?"

"Nothing. I just—"

I turn to him. Although the moon is illuminating his face, his brow ridge buries his eye sockets in shadow, making him look soulless. I know I should formulate my thoughts more before I start talking, but the word-vomit spews anyway.

"Sorry to backpedal, but just so we're clear . . . I think I would like to get married. Not soon or anything. I'd want to wait until *at least* after med school and my internship year, so the youngest I'd be is twenty-six. But from the sounds of it, you think marriage is setting yourself up for failure. And if you did do it, it wouldn't be until after you'd test-driven a bunch more girls so you can make an informed decision, right?"

Now Guy's stepping away, and his expression looks as if he just sucked a lemon.

"And, Guy, you have every right. But I need to know if that's your plan."

"*Plan?* Wh-what *plan*? There's no plan."

"Because if that's how you feel, then . . . we can't be together anymore."

Guy's jaw drops. "What am I missing here?" He looks to either side as if the answer could be hanging in the air. "I wasn't talking about *us* before. I was just telling you about my sociology class. We were, you know, shootin' the shit, or so I thought."

"So you didn't mean what you said?"

"Well—I—I didn't *not* mean it . . . but what does that have to do with anything?"

"Um, *everything*? We can't keep, you know, doing what we're doing unless we're on our way to being a couple."

"I'd say we're a couple. I haven't seen anyone else since *Star Wars*. I didn't—I don't—want to."

Right now, I'm more baffled than pleased by that admission.

"But . . . if you're my 'boyfriend,' you shouldn't be thinking about still playing the field one day—"

"Okay, hold up a sec. Now *my* head hurts." Guy rubs his temples with his hands. "Dom, you realize we're not even old enough to drink legally, right?"

"Yes, I get that this is premature." I catch my breath and

slow down. "All I mean is that, hypothetically, *if* we keep going out and we're happy, then why would we need to see anyone else? And *as long as* we're going out and happy, wouldn't marriage be . . . the goal, even if it's a decade away? 'Cause if it's not, all this is pointless."

Guy looks blankly toward the surf. Then he sits down on the sand and assumes the *Thinker* position. I take a seat, too, mortified that I brought up matrimony so early, when I never once discussed it with my ex in all the months we were together. Maybe I'm just on edge from the Gainesville commotion. Still, it feels right putting all this out in the open. Seventeen-year-old me would've stewed in silence in the hopes that any red flags would disappear on their own. But that rarely happens. And I simply won't turn a blind eye anymore.

Finally, Guy announces, "First of all, I get what you're saying. I mean, if two people are that positive they belong with each other, then, yeah, I guess it'd be illogical for them to be with anyone else."

I nod ardently, now sorry I became so intense.

"Second, I'm not *against* marriage, okay? But . . . it's a big freakin' deal. And I couldn't forgive myself if I screwed it up. So it wouldn't be until the distant future when I'm ready."

"That's fine. I'm the same way, really."

"But there's a more pressing issue." He stares gravely at me. "Dom, you know I think you're awesome, and this summer's been so much better with you in it. I'd like to keep seeing you—and *only* you—while you're here."

I stifle my grin. "So where's the 'issue' with that?"

He repeats slowly, "While you're *here*."

When his meaning registers a second later, it feels like a tornado sweeping through my heart. From day one Guy gave us an August expiration date, and here I was, daring to hope he could be my ever after. I cover my face with my hands, ashamed at how deluded I was not to detect earlier that he was too good to be true. How is it that two people can be in the same relationship and still have completely different ideas of what's going on?

"I'm sorry, Dom, but I thought that was a no-brainer. We can't stay together next semester if we're never going to *be* together. The phone's a crappy substitute for the real thing."

"*Believe me,* I get that geography's an obstacle. But people work through it, like Matt and Brie. And you're already half done with Ford."

"Yeah, but it's not like conditions will clear after graduation. What are the chances of your med school being near my grad school? And then what if I don't get work near where you match for residency? And you said at your place you wanted to do Doctors Without Borders. That could put you on a separate continent."

"Well . . . it's not *definite* I'll do Doctors Without Borders."

"*I want you to!*" He stands up and waves his arms. "That's just it—I want us both to do all the cool things we want, where we want, and not be held back by anything, or any*one*. And later, whenever our careers are solid and we've lived and all that crap, who knows what could happen?" He sits back down closer to me. "And even if you went to Ford, Dom, it'd still be hard to keep things going. I get so busy during the year with classes and Greek stuff. Girls just end up getting mad at me for not being 'available' enough."

"You mean, for not *making the effort* to be 'available' enough," I jab, suddenly understanding why Guy didn't already have a girlfriend when we met.

"C'mon, Dom. We're together *now,* and there's no one else I'd rather be with. Let's enjoy this while we have it."

I breathe and stiffly shake my head. "I just know myself, Guy. I can't be happy going out if it's not . . . going anywhere. We might as well cool it now."

I'm stunned that those words escape me, when minutes ago life was a fairy tale. I always thought you broke up with people because you didn't want to be with them. But I *do* want to be with Guy, so I'm dumping him so he can't dump me first. I recall that *Cosmo* article about third dates being the make-or-break moment for couples. Maybe that's rooted in hard science after all.

Guy falls back on his elbows and harrumphs in exasperation. After some more surf staring, he says, "Wow. This really sucks."

"I promised always to tell you what I'm thinking."

"I know. I'm glad you did. Well, I'm not *glad*." He sighs again. "Anyway, this totally stinks, but obviously I'll respect it. I won't lay a hand on you from now on."

" 'From now on'?"

"Well, whenever we hang out, and then there's that wedding." When I don't respond, he continues, "We're still hanging out, aren't we?"

"I . . . don't think . . . that'd be a good idea."

"Whoa, whoa, whoa." He stands up again and barks, "If you're not my girlfriend, fine. But that is *no* reason we have to be strangers. That's bullshit!"

I stand up, too, and glare at him indignantly. So it's all right for him to rule out a serious relationship, but it's wrong if I'm not ready to settle for less?

"Guy, I can't just . . . automatically switch modes. I need some space—"

"This is insane!" He stomps his foot. "We were hardly going out! You've never even let me French you!"

I lock my hands on my hips and shout, "What does *that* have to do with anything?"

He shouts louder, "You're making a problem where there isn't any!"

I scream, "I'm preventing bigger problems down the line!"

I've occasionally raised my voice to my parents, but I've never had it out with anyone like this before. And like most fights, it's all so stupid. The minutes we squander arguing can all be boiled down to Guy calling me impractical and me calling him insensitive, though I think both of us know neither of those things is true. We carry on until I notice a couple in the distance and demand that we leave before we completely humiliate ourselves. But as awful as yelling is, it's not nearly as tense as our wordless speed-walk back to his Accord, and the ten-mile drive home. Melodramatically enough, we pull up to my building at the stroke of midnight.

"So," he mumbles, "I guess you now think these last two weekends were pointless."

"No, Guy. I don't regret anything, if that's what you're after."

"I just wish I hadn't opened my big mouth when you mentioned Matt and what's-her-name."

"Actually, it's better this came up sooner rather than later." Otherwise, I *might* have regretted it.

Then he does one of those mini-laughs where you exhale quickly through your nose, and I ask him what's funny.

"That paper I wrote," he answers. "Entropy is true in life, too. In the end, everything turns to crap."

My stomach crumples. I want to tell him I'm sorry for how everything wound up and that maybe we can hang out again when enough time passes. I have no idea how long that'd be, though, and my throat's too tight to speak anyway, so I just spill out of the car and slog up to the front entrance. I'm hoping to hear him floor the gas pedal and vroom away like a spiteful man-child I'd be embarrassed to be associated with, but he stays put until the elevator opens and I go inside. I know it's to make sure I get in safely. There should be a law prohibiting boys who aren't good for you from acting nice, so it's easier to justify not being with them.

Once in my room, I text Amy what happened and ask her to call me if she's up. When I don't hear back, I lie awake in bed second-guessing my decision. But Guy and I see things too differently to keep dating. In the same way that a fiancée is a bride-to-be, I've always thought a girlfriend is a fiancée-to-be. Yes, most relationships bite the dust before things get long-term. However, that *possibility* of staying together forever remains the underlying force driving the relationship forward. To Guy, though, a girlfriend can merely be someone you go out with until it's inconvenient—in effect, a single-girl-to-be. That's not enough for me, so I suppose I did the right thing. It just sucks when being right means being alone.

When at five a.m. I still can't sleep, I try tiring myself out by reorganizing my drawers and bookshelves. Then I remember that's a waste of energy, since soon I'll be putting everything into boxes. Growing more somber by the second, I plop in front of my computer and check grades for the umpteenth time this vacation—nothing. Finally I log on to Facebook, where Tulane's head RA posted photos from the Bastille Day midnight mixer that just ended. I'm not surprised to see that Calvin dominates most of the pictures, striking silly poses on the main quad, and the one of him dangling from an oak tree limb makes me grin. But next I click to a shot of him sitting on the grass with an RA from the girls' dorm, and they're kissing.

Like a woman possessed, I pounce on my cell and start dialing.

11

"So, what do you care?" Amy asks groggily. "I never thought you'd call me at the crack of dawn over Calvin Brandon, *Coppertone*."

"Sorry I woke you, but I just don't get it! Cal hasn't looked twice at this girl before—*Samantha Finley*." I mutter her name while skimming her public profile. "Listen. Her interests are fashion, astrology, tattoos, and yoga. Cal hates all those things."

"They were only kissing."

"Yeah, in the pictures. Right now they could be screwing!"

"Then good for him! You gave him *no* reason to hold out

for you. Did you really expect he'd keep himself on standby in case you miraculously fell for him?"

"No, but . . . I don't know." Admittedly, not having a boyfriend is a lot less dejecting when there's a suitable prospect waiting in the wings. "Oh, Ames. Why *didn't* I fall for him?"

"*Because you didn't!*" Amy exclaims, understandably impatient. "*You're* the scientist here. You know attraction is all about liking each other's scents and gauging how the guy would've hunted if we still lived in caves. The Cal-man may be awesome, but he just doesn't do it for you."

I think back to how delicious Guy smells and his tall, strong physique. It's so messed up how little control we have over whether we want somebody.

"And, Dom, I still don't get why you chucked that Beta. He's a chance to have no-strings-attached fun! I love Joel to pieces, but sometimes I wish he hadn't come along until next year so *I* could enlist a few more hot summer flings."

"You know very well I'm not into random hookups, no offense."

"None taken, and Beta-boy's anything but 'random.' He's a good guy, and you genuinely like each other."

"I just don't see what's in it for me if he's only temporary. It'd be relationship suicide."

"Well, nothing lasts forever. Buddhist monks spend days constructing these intricate sand paintings called mandalas, only so they can destroy them afterward. The important thing is *making* the mandalas, not how long they last."

"Okay, Ames, but sand art's a tad different from love."

"You're *in love* already? It's been, like, nine days since you two met."

I exhale slowly. "No. I can't say I love Guy , . . . but that's the direction I hoped this would go."

Amy remains on the phone with me until I have to start getting ready for Lee County Medical, and I'm glad today's Monday so there's an entire workweek ahead to fill my time. Nevertheless, my internship feels routine now that I've been doing it for a couple of weeks, which is making it tougher to stay focused. My supervisor keeps promising that I'll be allowed to shadow doctors soon, but I still catch myself speculating about what could've been had I instead gotten a Res-Life stint as Calvin suggested. It couldn't be much duller than my clerical duties at the hospital. And perhaps by being near Calvin all day, our body chemistries would've naturally synced, and I'd have craved taking things to the next level with him.

I'm so disgusted with myself for obsessing over boys while surrounded by people suffering from infinitely worse problems. At Tulane we learned how females have extra white matter connecting different parts of the cerebrum. That's why women tend to be good multitaskers, which started as far back as the caveman era, when mothers had to juggle several thoughts at once in order to care for all their kids. But it also means I can do my work and feel bad for patients while still dwelling on relationships and feeling bad for *me*. The fact that I'm anatomically hardwired not to compartmentalize emotions doesn't make my state of mind any less deplorable.

I ride out the first half of the week without incident, and I'm grateful to my bratsitting kids for adding much-needed silliness to my days. Everyone keeps asking me if I'm okay, however, so my reaction to the Gainesville-Guy-Calvin triple whammy must be plain on my face. Then, by Wednesday,

I'm so spacey from not sleeping well that I completely forget to check grades until I'm about to go to bed. I tramp over to my computer and log on to the registrar, expecting to be taunted with another blank screen, so I do a double take when I see that they've finally been posted. Neuroscience: A. Biomedical Ethics: A-. My cumulative GPA is holding steady at 3.8, which means my merit scholarship is safe. I have everything I worked for and could've wanted. . . .

So how come I feel nothing?

I bet I'd be more excited if I could share the news, but tonight Amy's preoccupied at her own computer having another video chat date with Joel. As for my parents, they're huddled around the dining room table poring over printouts of Gainesville house listings, which are the last things I want to see right now. It's about time I call Calvin, especially because we haven't spoken since texting each other "Happy 4th of July" almost two weeks ago. But I feel like such a loser having nothing better to do than talk about exams, when he's probably naked in bed with Samantha. Next I log on to Facebook, and, just as I predicted, he has changed his status to "in a relationship" with her. Calvin must know I'm seeing this. . . .

Maybe he *wants* me to see it.

Or maybe he's not thinking about me at all. I hate how you can feel broken up with someone without ever having dated.

In a fit of self-pity, I switch to Guy's page. His latest post shows that he'll be going to the Midsummer Night's Rockfest, a free concert 101 FM is throwing this Friday. I bet he's going to have *so* much fun. That it's my choice not to join him won't make me less lonely. It's hard to believe, though, that we were dating just last weekend. It was all over so rapidly that Guy feels like a phantom. I decided not to unfriend him because it seemed mean to cut him off completely when he didn't do anything wrong. And like I told Amy, I didn't love him yet, so what I'm experiencing isn't exactly *heartbreak*. I don't loathe myself for not being loved by him, and thinking about him doesn't leave me in excruciating physical pain. I'm just disappointed. And disillusioned. Guy and I fit on so many levels, and given the chance, maybe it *could've* been love, and maybe it could've been for forever.

It all begs the question, though: Was my not loving Guy really because we knew each other for only a few days?

My parents claim they fell in love on the *first* day. . . .

Or was my not loving Guy because you can't fall for someone if you're still hung up on someone else?

Now devolving into full-out masochism, I run a Facebook search for the NYU track and field page so I can see my high school boyfriend's face among the team photos. *He* was a total heartbreak situation, which is why I keep his personal page blocked. I realize that's immature of me, considering we went through so much more together than Guy and I did—my ex and I were each other's first everything. But loving him had become like an addiction, so I figured the best way to beat it was to make a clean break. That's why I'm not tagging along with Amy to their high school track reunion this Friday. Even though she told me that *he* RSVP'd no to the Evite because he's in Manhattan working a summer job, I don't want to subject myself to the possibility of his old friends grilling me like Brie did, or hearing them talk about how he's doing better than I am. At least, I *presume* he's doing better. From his mile-wide smile in the pictures, it's doubtful he's home alone cyber-stalking *me*. That's the thing about exes—for eternity you feel like rivals in a kind of happiness contest, and losing would be the epitome of tragedy.

I switch off my monitor and crawl under the covers, knowing full well this will be another sleep-deficient night. Then I remember another thing *Cosmo* said. It typically takes half the time you're dating a guy to fall out of love with him. My ex and I were together almost ten months before he admitted over the holidays that he'd fallen out of love with me, so by that measure I should've been cured weeks ago. But once you've anticipated spending forever with someone, I'm not convinced you can ever feel complete after being uncoupled. I think you just learn to live without the person. Like when someone dies, you don't stop loving them just because they're not around to love you back anymore. Breakups truly are a kind of death. All year I plodded through the stages of mourning that I was just tested on in Biomedical Ethics—shock, anger, depression, and acceptance. The hitch, though, is that even when you've reached acceptance, you can sometimes regress so quickly, it's scary.

Like I did at the Braffs' barbecue.

Like I'm doing now.

I sit up and clutch my head in my hands. I have two options: I can distract myself from my ex—by reading, packing, or working out—or I can feed my addiction. It's obvious which one's right, and most of the time I go with it. Tonight, though, I trudge toward my linen closet, where I keep the big, bulky garbage bag that I filled with all my reminders of *him* on the night he dumped me.

I strew the bag's contents over my bathroom floor—
movie ticket stubs, a mood ring he gave me, dozens of framed
photos. The inventory goes on. Sure, seeing this stuff again
is torture. But it's soothing, too, because it's familiar. The
only difference is that now everything's coated with the
crumbled remains of my rose prom corsage, making it all appear as if it's been dug up from a grave, which I guess it has.

I study the pictures taken last summer, which are mostly
of our graduations, the Braffs' Independence Day barbecue,
and our joint going-away dinner before we left for college
in August—the beginning of the end. My eyes then land on
another August shot of us at his grandparents' fifty-ninth
wedding anniversary. It took place in their Captiva Island
vacation home, which lies vacant most of the year, and I
wince recalling all the times my ex and I would sneak away
there to get it on. I can't believe I wasn't more bothered then
by how disrespectful that was. I guess I was too busy thinking about how his grandparents also met during their senior year in high school, which in my mind meant that their
grandson and I were fated to follow in their footsteps. Serves
me right, for me, a wannabe doctor, to have relied on something as unscientific as destiny.

I continue foraging through the pile, and as I catch sight
of our half-empty condom box, I wonder about whether I
should bring all these things to Gainesville. It seems stupid
to, since, as far as I'm concerned, the sole benefit of moving is making a fresh start in a new place. I can't trash this,
though. It's the only concrete evidence left that we were once
a *we*—

"Just quit it!" I shout at myself.

I toss everything into the bag and hoist it back into the recesses of my linen closet.

All that's happening now is another "step back," which is normal, absolutely normal. But by wallowing, I'm flat-out *ensuring* he's doing better than me.

In an effort to clear my head, I strip off my pajamas, lie down in the bathtub, spread my knees, turn on the water, and position my hips so the stream lands on just the right spot. Then I close my eyes and sift through my mental catalog of hot men like Matt and Mr. Chesnoff, before settling on Guy. Next I'm visualizing us back at Bantam Beach, except now we're not avoiding *any* bases, and all the while Guy's raving that I'm the only girl for him. Soon I'm grasping the sides of the tub as spasms ripple through me. But it's all over seconds later. And when I open my eyes to turn off the faucet, the first thing I see is the ugly image of my three-day unshaven legs spread-eagle under a calcified waterspout. I begin bawling uncontrollably.

My main motive for coming back here this summer wasn't just to vacation or be with Amy. It was to enjoy living at home again despite its being the site where I was rejected. It was to stamp out hurtful memories by making happy and empowering ones. Meanwhile, Fort Myers isn't even *home* for much longer. I'm unwanted by every guy in my life. And now here I am, more than half a year post-breakup, and my latest "memory" is of trying to jolt myself out of my funk by getting off with the aid of modern plumbing. That's not *empowering*. It's *pitiful*.

I don't bother changing back into my pajamas before hurling my soaked, naked body into bed and sobbing myself to sleep.

12

I should've just called in sick. All Thursday, I'm so addled, I mess up the simplest tasks, like distributing the incoming mail and taking down the nurses' lunch orders. Bratsitting that night doesn't fare much better. With all my trembling, *I'm* the one spilling apple juice on my pants, which the five-year-old I'm watching thinks is hilarious because it looks like I peed myself.

But my crowning moment occurs Friday when I accidentally wheel the hospital library book cart into a loaded gurney, causing heavy hardcovers to fly off and thwack the patient on his suspended leg cast. I end up spending lunch hiding out in a janitor's closet, having another meltdown.

On top of feeling loveless and rootless, I'm incompetent, too. And to think I was wondering why my supervisor hasn't let me shadow doctors yet.

When I finally get home that evening, my parents are already on their way to Chez Jacques with their friends to celebrate moving to Gainesville. Mom left me my favorite grilled bass dinner to reheat, along with a congratulatory cupcake for getting good grades, but as is common in the depression stage of grief, I can't eat. Instead, I go straight to bed and close my eyes despite the fact that it's still light out and I'm wide-awake. I'm just biding my time until Amy comes over, which she texted should be around nine. But then she phones at seven.

"Hey," I answer sullenly. "Isn't your track reunion thing going on?"

"Yeah, but I skipped out early 'cause it was lame, so I'm heading to your place now." I hear her car engine start. "And you can stop freaking, because the answer is *no,* I didn't find out anything there about Mr. NYU."

"Good. I couldn't take it tonight if you heard he had a new girlfriend. This has been my shittiest week in a while. I didn't tell you before, but . . . a couple days ago I looked through the ex bag."

"Ugh, Dom!" she heaves. "You are *so* beyond this. It's time you get rid of that junk!"

"That's easier said than done. And I don't *like* being this screwed up, Ames. I'm as tired of it as you are. But with so much not going my way, I can't help it."

"Well, enough feeling bad about him. *All* hims. Feel bad for *me.* I just wasted an hour of my life!"

"Bummer the party wasn't fun. I thought you were tight with a lot of those trackies."

"Emphasis on 'were.' And what blows is that I was so psyched about seeing everyone again, but with the few people who did show, none of us meshed anymore. I mentioned Rauschenberg, and not one of them expressed interest in coming to any shows, and that's after I rooted for all their asses at every single meet in high school. I just had to get outta there."

I'm usually a homebody, but as Amy rattles on about how everything's changing, I'm now dreading staying in for another of our tween-style sleepovers. Inevitably it'll make me more nostalgic for our pre-college days, which will further put me over the edge. If I'm ever going to pull myself out of this, I have to do something different. *Feel* something different.

Then, as if my body were acting on its own, I go to my desk and bring up Guy's Facebook page. Just minutes ago Bruce "checked in" himself, Guy, and three other boys—whose names I recognize from Guy's stories as Betas—at the Midsummer Night's Rockfest, that free concert Guy posted about earlier. . . .

Why am I not there with him, again?

Around Guy, I felt energized and stimulated and *happy,* and now I'm denying myself him and getting nothing in return. And no one can blame Guy for steering clear of commitments. I've tried the love thing, and if it implodes, you're damaged for life. In the meantime, I've been so caught up with mapping out a picture-perfect "forever" that I'm completely neglecting my present, which I have far more control over anyway.

Suddenly I flash back to more than a decade ago, when I started going to sleepaway camp. Each summer there was invariably one girl I became inseparable with, but after our families picked us up and school resumed, we almost always lost touch. I'm still glad those friendships happened even though nothing came from them. Summer would've been a lot less fun otherwise. And Amy's right. Everything ends eventually, including our bodies. I'd never tell a terminally ill patient to commit suicide just because death was imminent. I'd advise the patient to live it up in whatever time was left.

The Midsummer Night's Rockfest is being held at Seminole Field. That's just south of Ford and not far by car. As I click back to Guy's page and admire his handsome head shot, I sense stirring inside me that same spontaneous desire that prompted me to ask Guy out in the first place—that drive to take action instead of waiting for something to happen. And it makes me feel alive.

". . . I know that it's been a while since I hung out with the trackies, so I guess it was dumb to think we'd just pick up where we left off. Maybe I'm really not the same person I was back in high school. Or maybe *they're* not the same people—"

"Forget about them." I cut Amy short before running to the bathroom and laying out a new razor in my shower. "How do you feel about meeting some *new* people tonight?"

PART III

13

Despite heavy Friday-night traffic, Amy and I arrive at Seminole Field with ten minutes to spare before showtime. It's almost dark, and I can barely see any grass, there're so many people and picnic blankets. I had planned to text Guy that I'm here, but Amy claims I'll lose my courage to see him if he writes back something unenthusiastic or doesn't answer at all. She's probably right, so we begin weaving through the crowd to hunt him down. Then, as we're speeding by the concessions stands, I hear his voice.

"Dom Baylor?"

My heart rate skyrocketing, I skid to a stop, eye Amy,

and turn around. Guy's just standing there by himself, holding a soft pretzel, his mouth in an adorable O of surprise.

"Hey!" I exclaim, the delight in my voice impossible to mask. "Great to see you!"

"Oh. Um . . . yeah. You too," he says uncertainly as I step toward him. For a moment I consider playing off my being here as a coincidence, but the truth flies out.

"Actually, Guy, believe it or not, I was *hoping* to run into you."

He lifts his head and squints down at me with suspicion. After a silence he responds, "No kidding?"

"Yeah. Bruce posted online that you all were here, so I . . ." My voice trails off and I wink at him. He doesn't say anything, though the slow upward curl of his lips kills all the ugliness that has weighed on me since Sunday at Bantam Beach. "So," I continue, "are you with *just* the Betas?" Translation: *Did you bring a girl?*

"Right, it's only us dudes tonight. Well, not anymore." He stares me up and down, sending me into momentary light-headedness. "But why didn't you call?"

I shrug and quote him, " 'The phone's a crappy substitute for the real thing.' "

"Touché." He's still grinning.

"I was afraid, though, I wouldn't find you in this mob. It's lucky you spotted me."

"Well, your Lilith hair is hard to miss."

"Oh, yeah." I run my fingers through my ponytail, still damp from the shower. "You know, only, like, one in a hundred people have the melanocortin-1 receptor on their sixteenth chromosome that causes this color."

He laughs. "I always suspected you were a genetic mutation."

"It's true! At the hospital, a nurse told me that some redheads need extra anesthesia because—"

"*Ahem.*" Amy clears her throat. I forgot she was here!

"Oh, sorry! Ames, this is Guy Davies. Guy, Amy Braff."

"Heya, Guy!" Amy greets him with her megawatt smile, but Guy just nods at her before turning his gaze back to me. I'm such a Plain Jane next to Amy's bee-stung lips and curvaceous figure, and I'm used to guys ignoring me for her. It's fun being in her position this time.

The three of us then walk over to Guy's four frat brothers, who've staked out a space near the front of the field. En route I get nervous that they've heard about our fight and will be inclined to dislike me. But when we all introduce ourselves, everyone's friendly. Maybe Guy didn't tell them anything. I guess nothing we did really qualifies as news— short-lived relationships are a dime a dozen in college. Or it could be they're acting nice because Amy's here, back in her element as the center of attention. While the other Betas buzz around her, Guy and I share his pretzel and gab as if nothing ever happened.

"Work's been hell this week," Guy says. "The mainframe crashed, and we lost a bunch of data."

"It's been rough at the hospital, too. I tried so hard making friends with the med students, but they don't even acknowledge my existence."

"I know what you mean. The postdocs never let me forget I'm the low man on the totem pole."

"Oh, well. One day we'll show 'em who's boss—"

The floodlights flash on. Immediately, dozens of people stampede past us to rush the stage, leaving Amy and me unable to see the band over all the upraised arms. I don't really mind, since I didn't come for the music, but Amy's annoyed. Then I notice her shouting something into Bruce's ear. Five seconds later she's sitting up on his shoulders and tousling his hair as if she doesn't already have a boyfriend.

I'm torn between being awed and appalled by her, when Guy points to them and yells to me over the opening song, "WE CAN DO THAT, TOO."

"OH." I look back at him. "I DON'T KNOW."

"WHY? DON'T YOU WANT TO SEE?"

The sensible course of action would be for Guy and me to keep some physical distance until we discuss what's going on with us. I'm also perspiring from the July heat (and from seeing Guy), and I don't want to sweat all over him. Plus, I'd feel bad impeding the view of the people behind us. . . . On the other hand, if being sensible were my aim, I'd have just stayed home.

Guy makes puppy-dog eyes and extends his lower lip. "C'MON. YOU'RE MISSING EVERYTHING."

"OKAY." I smile. "WHY NOT?"

"ALL RIGHT!"

Guy kneels behind me and instructs me to spread my legs. After hesitating for a second because the whole thing feels so unreal, I obey. Guy then pokes his head out from between my thighs, and I hold in my giggles when I think how it would look to everyone if he were turned around. Finally I grab on to his hands and crouch forward.

"HANG ON TIGHT!"

Guy shoots up, and I shriek as the earth sinks beneath me.

"YOU OKAY UP THERE?" he asks, now standing upright.

"UM . . ." I remain frozen for a couple seconds until I'm confident we're stable. Then I slowly straighten out my back and breathe. "THE AIR'S A LITTLE THIN," I kid, letting go of his hands. "BUT I'M FINE."

"CAN YOU SEE?"

I pan the field with my eyes. "UH-HUH. PERFECTLY!"

Guy then passes up a Coors he disguised by cutting open a Coke can and pasting it over the beer can. I never understood the appeal of alcohol, though the whole concert atmosphere makes me thirsty for it in the same way you crave s'mores around a campfire or popcorn at the movies. So I pull open the tab and take a big slug. The taste is as revolting as ever, like liquid wood. But that toasty feeling as it runs down my throat is kind of nice. Now I look over to Amy, who gives me a high five, and for no good reason I start whooping at the sky. Nobody would guess that I'm the same person who forty-eight hours ago was crying naked in a tub.

After handing the can back down to Guy, I close my eyes, take slow breaths, and concentrate on relaxing. I try blocking out everything except the music, breeze, salty air, and Guy's calloused fingers gripping my ankles. With every passing minute I'm getting more in the moment, and soon it's as though I'm having a quiet epiphany about how good things really are. I'm young and free and on vacation and next to my BFF on this perfect midsummer's night, with a pack of boys as a bonus. How could I have ever dreamed of feeling sorry for myself?

Perhaps it's just the beer mellowing me out, but this is the first time in a long time that my mind's not racing, mulling, preparing, or strategizing. For once I don't care about *was* or *will* and just let myself *be*.

14

After the concert, Amy launches into her scheme to give Guy and me some time alone. First she suggests we all go to Chamber, a new eighteen-and-up club in North Fort Myers. Everyone seems into it, so then I lie about being too tired to join them. I'm not sure what we would've done next if Guy didn't offer to drive me home, but he does. By midnight, Amy's pulling out of Seminole Field with the other four Betas crammed into her Camry, while Guy and I commence the short walk to Ford's campus to retrieve his Accord.

I guess neither of us wants to confront what happened between us, since we're sticking to neutral subjects like what we thought of the concert and our favorite bands. Then, when we reach the Beta house driveway, all conversation grinds to a halt as we gawk at Guy's car. It seems to be repelling us with invisible currents to keep us from getting in.

"I was thinking, Dom . . ." Guy purses his lips in mock solemnity. "Maybe we should hold off a little longer before I get behind the wheel. I *was* boozing it up tonight."

Guy had only one drink, and that was hours ago, but I play along anyway.

"Maybe you're right. Better safe than sorry."

"Yeah. I bet your parents would prefer that we stall here for a while, since I'll be transporting precious cargo." He grins mischievously.

It feels *so* good flirting with him again. Then a completely insane idea comes to me that right now couldn't be more perfect. "If you want, Guy, I can run some medical tests on you to check whether the alcohol's out of your system."

"Like what? You carry a Breathalyzer around?"

I laugh. "No, I mean the psychophysical exercises that cops make drivers do when they suspect they've been drinking. My dad showed me back when I got my license. That way we can scientifically assess whether you're a true DUI risk."

"Hmm." He nods. "Okay . . . but only if you test me *inside* the house."

That's exactly what I was hoping he'd say.

When we get to the living room, I order Guy to take nine steps, heel to toe, in a straight line starting with his right foot.

"And when you get to nine, you have to swivel around

without taking your front foot off the ground. Then repeat everything going in the opposite direction. You also have to count the steps aloud as you take them, and you can't ever pause or use your arms for balance."

"That was a lot to remember," he says when he finishes. "I was really trying, and I still messed up the turn."

"That's okay. You have to get at least two things wrong to fail the test, so you would've passed."

Then I instruct him to stand motionless with one of his legs extended six inches off the ground.

"Hold it like that for thirty seconds, and count aloud. Be sure not to sway, hop, put your foot down, or rely on your arms."

"Damn!" he exclaims after stumbling midway. "This is hard even if you're sober. Winos don't stand a chance."

"That's the whole point."

Finally I approach him so we're just a few inches apart, and I hold up my index finger to the level of his eyes. I can almost hear my blood surge from facing him this closely again.

"For the last test, keep looking at my finger as I move my hand from side to side. If your eyes start jerking involuntarily, that's a sign you're under the influence of something."

I shift my finger to his left, but Guy's not following it. Instead he's staring straight down at me.

"Guy! Willful defiance of police orders would be grounds for me to arrest you."

"That doesn't sound so bad."

He begins bending over, and I tense up, certain he's about to kiss me. Instead he keeps moving down until he's kneeling. Then he presses the side of his face to my stomach and whimpers, "It's so cool you're here. I freakin' missed you."

I'm tempted to reply *Not enough,* because if I were really so special to him, he would've tracked me down to say he'd changed his mind and wanted to give our relationship a shot. It's useless arguing any more about impossibilities, though, so I just dig my fingers into his 'fro and say, "I missed you, too, Guy."

"I'm so sorry for . . . I don't know what. Sunday was awful."

"I'm sorry, too. I wish we could redo it."

"I still don't get what happened."

I sigh. "We disagreed."

"Yeah." He looks up at me. "Then . . . why'd you come tonight?"

"I guess because nothing says we can't . . . agree to disagree."

"Can we?" He gets back on his feet and smiles hopefully. "You're cool with hanging out again?"

"Apparently so," I answer, unconcerned that just five days ago I was positive that'd be the worst idea ever. Now I care only that this is the best I've felt since then.

"So, to clarify . . . you're cool with *just* hanging out?"

I turn away to hide my blushing. Then I hear myself tell him, "As long as I'm in Fort Myers, I see no need to impose limits."

Guy's tone gets serious. "How about everything you said before?"

I just shrug, but he goes on, "This is important, Dom. You're positive you're okay with, you know, us . . . not . . . after the summer?"

This time I'm tempted to reply, *Of course not, dummy!* But all he asked was if I'm "okay" with it. He's not asking if it's my dream scenario, which might never come true anyway. I'd rather be with Guy in the real world than by myself, fantasizing about some idealized version of our relationship. Because that's all ideals are—fantasies.

"Actually, I'm *more than* okay with it. Maybe I even kind of see your point."

And with that, Guy clasps his arms around my ribs and throws me over his shoulder like a backpack. I've been on his shoulders a lot tonight.

"Ahh!" I scream-laugh while flailing my legs. "What are you doing?"

"What does it look like?"

Holding tightly to my calves, Guy gallops up the stairs and down the hall to his room. Then he slams the door behind us, plunks me on his bed, and climbs on top of me. For a moment he just runs his hands over my hair and the length of my arms, as if to check that I'm real. Then he lowers his head to mine.

"Hello again," he says, breathing heavily from his mad dash up here.

"Hello."

We begin kissing, but I can tell he's fighting to hold back. So am I. I think about how my reasons for taking things slow with him don't apply to us anymore.

"Guy . . . what I said just now about limits . . . It's fine if we . . . speed this up—"

"For real?" His eyes brighten.

"I mean, for tonight, we probably shouldn't do *too* much, but—"

Glphf!

I nearly choke as his tongue clogs my throat. It's as though my teeth are going through a car wash. My chin feels like it's being pumiced to the bone by his beard stubble. *God, I missed this!*

A moment later Guy pulls up a little, and I can barely make out a thin thread of saliva bridging our lips.

"You okay?" he asks, the thread breaking.

"Fabulous!" I proclaim before clenching the nape of Guy's neck and pulling him back down to me.

I assumed that, after so many months of being without a boy, I might not remember how to French, but that basic motion of opening and closing our mouths in tandem is like second nature. It helps that Guy's an expert kisser—forceful and aggressive, yet still gentle and playful. I suppose he's had a lot of practice.

I also thought that making out with Guy wouldn't feel as nice now that I know we're done for. Back in high school, I never understood how Amy could enjoy getting with guys just for the short haul. In a way, though, making out like this is *more* enjoyable because there's no pressure for me to not do or say anything stupid. What's the worst that can happen if I do? So I'm freer to focus on what *I'm* feeling, not what *he* feels about me. I never appreciated before how much I was always putting myself second.

Soon I'm pushing Guy off.

"I'm sorry," I pant as if I just swam a mile. "I need a break. It's like I'm out of shape."

He laughs and wipes his mouth with his knuckles. "That's fine. Take five."

I also need to pee, so I excuse myself and head next door to the hall bathroom. I'd be more repulsed by its mildewy stench and carpet of pubes if I weren't so amazed that I'm mid-hookup with one of the finest guys in Florida. Then, as I'm washing my hands, the ringtone for my parents' landline blares on my cell. They wouldn't be calling this late unless something were wrong.

"Yeah?" I answer anxiously.

"Oh, thank God!" Dad wheezes. Then I hear him mumble to Mom that I'm fine.

"Dad, you okay? What's going on there?"

"I woke up with indigestion from that damn French restaurant your mother and I had dinner at, so I went to the living room to watch TV, and I saw your door was open and you weren't here."

"So? I'm hanging out with Guy. He was at the concert I texted you that I was going to with Amy."

"Fine, but it's after one. It looks like *someone* forgot her curfew."

I almost drop the phone.

"Um, actually, Dad, it looks like *someone* forgot I'm no longer in high school."

"It looks like *someone* forgot she's now living with her parents."

"It looks like *someone* forgot I can stay out as late as I want in college."

"It looks like *someone* forgot Fort Myers can be a dangerous city after hours, and her folks sleep a lot better knowing she's safe in her room."

"It looks like *someone* forgot it's completely unfair

that I have to be back at the same time I did when I was a minor!"

"Mmm. . . . All-righty, Dom. You have a point. From now on curfew's one-thirty."

"*One-thirty?* That's, like, right now."

"Which means *someone* had better start heading back ASAP. See you soon, hon."

Dad hangs up, which is lucky—otherwise I might've snapped that the sobriety tests *someone* taught me just came in handy as foreplay. I realize that my parents worry because they love me and that they get to call the shots as long as I'm under their roof. Between this and the move, though, I'm really beginning to resent them.

Guy's totally chill when I explain the situation, but as I stand to leave, he says, "Before I take you back, do you mind if I come first?"

"Hmm? Come where?"

He smiles like he's holding in a laugh. Then he glances down at his shorts.

"Oh!" I clasp my fingers over my mouth and try not to laugh, either.

"The thing is, Dom, I don't want to risk blue balls. That hurts like a mother."

"Uh . . . well . . ." I'm still swallowing giggles. "Of course I don't want you to be in pain, but Dad's waiting up for me."

"I can be quick when I have to."

I have no problem saying no to him. Even if Guy gets any discomfort, I've read that it will disappear eventually. But since I'm already late, I suppose another few minutes won't make a difference, so I tell him it's fine.

I assume he'll go to the bathroom, or that he'll ask me to wait downstairs. Instead he springs back onto the bed, undoes his fly, and reaches for my right hand. "Wanna help the cause?"

I've given my ex dozens of hand jobs in the past, so none of this is foreign to me. Still, I wasn't expecting any nakedness tonight, and I sense my whole body seizing up.

"Sorry, Dom. Is this too fast?"

"Well, more like too sudden. I just—"

"It's cool. I'll be only a minute."

Guy then hikes up his T-shirt and pulls down his shorts and briefs so swiftly, I don't have a chance to see his whole penis before he grabs hold of it and starts stroking furiously. I cover my mouth again, astonished he's actually doing this *in front of* me. I couldn't imagine touching myself with anyone else watching. It just seems so private, like going to the bathroom. But Guy doesn't appear the least bit self-conscious, which is doubly impressive since what he's doing isn't exactly attractive. How is it that human anatomy evolved so that something as stupid-looking as a repetitive back-and-forth movement can generate the peak of physical ecstasy?

Guy wasn't exaggerating about being fast. In a matter of seconds he's grunting and convulsing. By the light of the lava lamp, it looks like his chest is being squirted with neon-green silly string.

After it's over, Guy reaches for some tissues, which is when I get my first unobstructed view of him. Even in the dark it's clear he's bigger than my ex. That something so unimportant can make me so thrilled is absurd. Nonetheless, I feel like I definitely gained the lead in the exes happiness contest, and a smug grin coils across my face for the entire car ride back to my building.

"You'd better go in now," Guy says when we pull in front of the entrance. "I don't want you to get *grounded*."

I shake my head. "Mom and Dad are being *so* ridiculous. There've been plenty of times when I've come home for school breaks this year and stayed out past one, and they never found out, 'cause they were asleep. And if Dad's that concerned with Fort Myers being dangerous, why'd he even let me go to Tulane, which is in the most dangerous city in the country?"

"I think it's a law of nature that parents are unreasonable, and it's harder to take the older we get. When I went home last summer, mine drove me so crazy, I almost ran away. That's why I kept my distance this summer. I will next summer, too."

I wonder if this will be my last summer with my parents as well. I don't know whether I'm relieved or sad at that prospect.

"Well, thanks for the lift, Guy."

"Thanks for coming out."

Guy leans over, cups my face in his hands, and kisses me until my whole mouth numbs.

"FYI," I gasp while floating out of his car, "the invitation's still open for that wedding next month, if you're free."

"I think that can be arranged. Oh, and I still have your Herophilus book. I haven't had time to read it yet. When I finished, I *was* just gonna drop it off at the front desk at your hospital, but—"

"Now you won't have to." I smile, glad to know that I'll

be seeing the book again after all. Before tonight, I'd written it off as breakup damages.

Back upstairs, I fill out Matt and Brie's RSVP card for two attendees. As I drop it down the mail slot, I think how, by Guy's definition anyway, I have a boyfriend again, and *our* curfew is in five weeks.

15

"Bruce kissed me at Chamber last night," Amy announces over breakfast at IHOP, where I'm wolfing down scrambled eggs as if my life depended on it. It's remarkable how ravenous hooking up can make you. "But I pulled away and told him I had a boyfriend. He didn't seem pleased."

"Well, you *were* pretty touchy-feely at the concert, so maybe that gave him the impression you *wanted* him to kiss you."

"Whatever. All that matters is I didn't kiss back, though it was tough not to. That Bruce is one fine frat boy."

"Are you going to tell Joel?"

"Why should I? It was a one-way snog that I intercepted on contact. There's no sin to confess." She takes a bite of her hash browns and smirks. "It's not like I watched him beat off or anything."

We both bust up again.

"I still can't believe how casual Guy was about that."

"Well, he's obviously very secure in his sexuality and probably incredible in the sack, which means you're in for quite the summer. First you study biology, now *Guy*-ology. Eek! I'm so stoked—you're gonna be 'taking a *luv-ah*.' "

"Or not. I'm fine just fooling around with him. And just because I've done it with one boy doesn't mean I'm obligated to do it with everyone else I go out with."

"True, but if *I* became single again, I don't think abstinence would be in the cards anymore. Once you've ridden the roller coaster, the Ferris wheel's kinda restricting. And with Beta-boy, maybe you'll finally *like* doing the deed."

"I liked it before."

Amy raises an eyebrow.

"I'm not lying, Ames. I loved the closeness of it."

"You know what I mean. Sometimes when I'm with Joel, oh, my God, it feels so brain-spinningly fantastic I think I'm going to croak. The only thing that replicates it is the vibrator I bought when he started camp. It's much better than the wand massager I used before. But it's still not as fun as actually being with him—"

"*Thank you* for those lovely images." I look around us to make sure no one's listening in. "And it's not that I wouldn't like to do it with Guy. I think all the time about how it'd be with him. But I don't know if it's worth going there at this point. It's already more than halfway through July, and we all know what happens next month."

"But aren't rebounds supposed to be quick? Anyway, everyone says that the best way to get *over* someone is to get *under* someone else. This could be your next 'experiment.'"

"Yeah, 'cause my Cal one turned out *so* awesome for me."

"Well, whatever you decide, I'm just glad you and Beta-boy kissed and made *out*. 'Cause, actually"—she shifts on the booth cushion and strokes her locket—"Joel asked me to visit again next weekend, and now that you have a playmate, I'll feel a lot less guilty about skipping town."

I gulp down my orange juice and try to smile for her. I'm unsuccessful.

"Of course you can come with me," Amy continues, "but then you'd have to leave your *toy*friend. And after last night, it'll be good for me to catch up on some couple's time with Joel if we're gonna make it until Matt and Brie-*dzilla* say 'I do.' Being apart brings too many temptations. I gotta remember to pack bug spray, though. . . ."

I wish I could be happy about her trip. Instead I'm distraught that at the rate everything's going, this will probably be my last summer with my best friend, and it's not even a whole summer. None of this is shocking, though. It's yet another example of how the person you're physical with takes priority, and I'm just as bad. When Amy asks if we're having a sleepover later, I tell her I already made plans to stay late at Guy's. She completely understands.

After Guy answers the Beta house door that evening, we barely say hello to each other before we're back in his bed. At first it irks me that his brothers are just down the hall, but so what if they assume we're hooking up? It's true, and there's no shame in it. I even feel an illicit thrill from them knowing that there's more to me than the grade-grubber most people pigeonhole me as. It makes me extra eager to take things further with Guy, which he must perceive, because after only a few minutes of kissing, I feel his right hand slither up my arm and over my collarbone before settling over my right breast.

"This cool so far?" he asks while gliding his hand to my left one.

"Well . . . my shirt loves it, but I don't feel a thing," I reply with a boldness I didn't know I was capable of.

"Okay." He laughs. "I get the hint."

Guy begins unlacing my peasant blouse. I'm also wearing a camisole and bra, despite it being ninety degrees outside. Even though I already counted on us shedding our clothing tonight, I wanted to have on as many layers as possible to give myself extra time to back out in case I started having doubts.

A minute later Guy easily unclasps my bra but pauses without moving the straps. It's my final chance to object, but I still have no impulse to stop. I'm glad I prolonged this whole process, though. A boy sees a girl topless for the first time only once, and the anticipation of the big reveal is really exciting. I feel like I'm a present being unwrapped. I nod for Guy to go ahead. He slowly draws the bra off.

Then he just grins for a moment before tearing off his own shirt, lunging downward like a hawk, and sucking my nipples. It's wrong that an act meant for nursing infants should feel this good. Next, he nestles his nose in between my breasts and motorboats away, which doesn't feel as good as it does gratifying. Of all the far more endowed girls in Fort Myers, Guy's choosing to do this with *me*. Soon we're Frenching again while Guy kneads both my breasts with his hands, and I'm getting so turned on, I yank down his cargo shorts and let him slip off my capris, which also takes him a while, since I purposely wore my pair with a button fly. When he starts fiddling with the hem of my panties, I wait for my conscience to flood with misgivings about exposing my crotch to a boy I've known for only two weeks. Instead I feel myself nodding once more, and suddenly I'm nude.

But then Guy switches on his bed lamp.

"Guy! No!" I grab the pillow and hold it over my torso.

"Yikes. Sorry, Dom." He turns off the lamp, leaving the green lava globs as the only light source. "I didn't mean to upset you. I just wanted to see you better."

"I know. I'm not mad. I just prefer it dark."

"Okay, that's cool . . . but may I ask why?"

I never gave it much thought before, but doesn't everyone make out in the dark? I always did, at least when I was undressed. It just feels less exploitative than with light, which showcases every stray hair my razor missed, those ugly little bumps on my areolas, and the uglier stretch marks I got spring semester from working off the freshman fifteen I packed on in the fall.

"I guess I just feel . . . sexier with the lights off."

"But you're gorgeous, Dom!"

"Thanks," I say weakly.

"That's it. I'm staging an intervention. Don't wig out."

Guy turns the lamp back on but angles the bulb toward

the wall so it's still dim. Then he jumps up out of bed and stands before the full-length mirror hanging on his closet door. He waves his hand for me to follow.

"Really, Guy. This is unnecessary."

"Why don't you look for just . . . ten seconds? I'll even time it. Please?"

He makes his cute puppy-dog eyes again, and I reason that the quickest way to get out of this is to comply. "Fine," I drone, throwing off the pillow. "Start counting."

"One Mississippi . . ."

It feels like déjà vu. Growing up, I'd spend hours naked before my own full-length mirror to monitor how I was developing. But once I got to Tulane last August, I don't think I ever saw my reflection without at least a towel on. What with having a roommate and sharing a hall bathroom, there was never a chance to. That may be why it's so easy in college to get fatter without realizing it until your clothes stop fitting. Then after my breakup in December, I avoided looking in mirrors any longer than I had to. I felt so disgusted about losing my boyfriend and gaining the weight that I couldn't face myself. I wish my ex could see me now, though, because I am pretty fit again. And Guy doesn't seem repelled by all my imperfections. If anything, in this light we resemble the people on the covers of Amy's collection of erotica novels, where a bare-chested he-man type stares lustily at a breathy maiden.

". . . ten Mississippi," Guy finishes, but I don't move away. Instead I turn to the side to admire my profile. I understand now that the appeal of flings isn't just that they're fun—they also build your self-esteem. Nothing makes you get down on yourself and worry that you're undesirable like rejection, so having someone desirable desire you is the ultimate antidote. And aphrodisiac.

I spin around to Guy and practically slam his hand against my breast before tumbling with him onto the bed. Soon I let my knees fall open so he can roll on top of me.

"But we—we can't do it," I stammer between kisses. "At least not tonight. Maybe never. I'd like to, but—"

"It's okay, Dom. We don't need it."

Then, with nothing but his boxers separating us, he starts slowly rocking against me. It's so nice, I almost forget to breathe.

"*This* cool so far?" he asks while licking my chest.

I nod as familiar tremors build up inside me that make me writhe and arch my back. "Ohs" and "yeahs" soar from my lips, and the tremors now coalesce into the sensation of a tidal wave building up down there. Guy revs up his speed, and he's so hard, I'm astounded he hasn't punctured through his underwear. Finally I wrap my legs around him tightly, coaxing the wave to swell higher, and higher.

I grab Guy's pillow again, this time to hold it over my mouth so my voice won't carry. It doesn't end up mattering, though, because Guy comes shortly after me and does nothing to muffle his moans, which sound like a savage animal being sacrificed. The priss in me wants to tell his brothers that we didn't have sex and were only dry-humping. I nearly laugh thinking how funny that would sound: *We were only dry-humping!*

"Wow," Guy says, peeling off his now-drenched boxers and tossing them onto the floor. "It was *so* hot watching you come."

That's the strangest compliment I've ever received. "Seriously?"

"Yeah. Normally I can hold off a lot longer, but seeing you lose yourself like that . . . Man, it drove me wild." Guy lies back down next to me. "I felt bad last night that I was the only one getting off, so today I'm glad things were 'equal.'" He winks.

I'm about to tell him something, but I hesitate because it's really personal. It seems silly, though, holding back with someone when we're already seeing each other stark naked and at our most vulnerable. I suppose that's the whole genesis behind pillow talk.

"You know, Guy, that was actually, um, the first time I've ever . . . come in front of anyone."

"Oh, really? Well, I'm glad I was able to make you. I find every woman's a little different in that way."

"*Oh, really?* And, pray tell, how many 'women' are you basing your deduction on?"

He shrugs. "I'm pretty sure they wouldn't want me to say anything."

"I'm not asking for names, Guy. And I'm entitled to know your sex stats before we go any further." I jostle his shoulders. "Just tell me. How many girls?"

"Okay, but define 'sex.' Are you talking broadly speaking or standard P in V?"

"Um . . . both."

"All right. Uh . . ." He crosses his hands behind his head and thinks for a moment. "Regular sex: five. Oral: I don't know . . . Maybe three or four more? And this is all spread out since tenth grade."

"You player," I tease. "Actually, that's not as many as I

would've guessed. I thought frat boys were all about getting as much ass as possible."

"Well, I have no interest in being with ditzes or bitches, and that really narrows my options, even at Ford."

"Aw, poor baby." I lie on my side and twiddle his chest hair with my fingers. "And in the spirit of full disclosure, I've done it with only one boy. I used to think I'd hold out until I was married or at least in my twenties, but that all changed senior year."

"I would hope. As an anatomy-phile, you should be in on doing it."

"I don't know how 'in on' it I am. Before you, I'd never even hooked up with anyone besides my ex, and he'd never been with anyone before, either."

"Aha. *That's* the reason it was never good with him. The poor dude just didn't know what he was doing." He shakes his head dolefully. "I've been there."

"*Neither* of us knew what we were doing. I didn't even figure out how to make *myself* come until after we split up, and I was just trying to feel something other than the pain."

"Day-um! I had whacking off nailed when I was thirteen. You must've been happy to finally know what you were missing with him."

"Yeah, but I honestly didn't care about all that when we were going out. You know, I was in love, yada, yada, yada."

Guy's face registers no reaction. After a pause, I ask him something I've been curious about since we met. "Have *you* ever been in love?"

He sighs. "Well . . . define 'love.' "

"Okay, if you have to ask, that's a *no*."

"Hmm . . . When I was a freshman in high school, I asked this cute junior in physics club to homecoming, but she said I was too young for her. I had a really bad headache for the rest of the day. Is that close?"

"Your head hurt for a *day*? That's hardly a crush! Love is . . . needing to be with this one person. No—it's more like *wanting* to need to be with this one person. Last semester my English professor read us this great Robert Frost quotation that went something like, 'Love is the irresistible desire to be irresistibly desired.'"

His eyebrows bunch. "I think you lost me."

"Okay. Your love interest becomes *the* most important thing to you. And if the love is requited, it's the biggest high in the universe, and you'd be fine never being with anyone else. But if this person doesn't want you back, well, you pretty much wish you were dead . . . or that that person dies miserable."

"Um, I think that'd go against the Hippocratic oath, Doc Baylor."

"Obviously, you don't *act* on those thoughts. It's just that terrible stuff goes through your mind because you're hurting so badly."

"You make love sound like hate."

"Well, it can be sometimes. They're both types of passion, and love can become hate, depending on what your love interest does."

"Aren't you getting love confused with, I don't know . . . infatuation?"

"There's a thin line there, too. In neuroscience, our textbook showed how the brain scans of people newly in love look a lot like the brain scans of patients with obsessive-compulsive disorder. In each case, your dopamine is suppressing your serotonin."

He laughs. "So essentially, love's a gnarly chemical cocktail that mimics mental illness."

"It's not always dramatic and crazy, though. In the best relationships, everything settles down after a while. And when things are going well, Guy, I swear to you"—I look away from him and stare out his window—"there's *no* beating being in love. It's as if you're in paradise on Earth . . . until things go bad."

"I'll take your word for it, but I don't know if it's for me. Maybe like how some people can't be hypnotized, some people can't fall in love."

"Don't speak too soon." I look back to him. "Amy used to doubt it'd ever happen to her before she met her boyfriend at Amherst."

"Uh-huh. Well, Bruce never would've guessed Amy was 'in love' last night. I thought she was cool and all, but the guys today were calling her a tease."

Like a shot, I sit up and yap, *"Oh, really? Then you can pass along this message to them from me."* I clutch Guy's arm and give him an Indian burn.

"Ow! Jesus!"

"You can also say that Amy would *never* talk shit about them." I turn away and pull up the blanket. Little does Guy know that I agree with his brothers.

"Sorry, Dom. I didn't want you to think Bruce was a dick for making a play for her. He just didn't know she had a boyfriend. It's a code of Beta that other dudes' girlfriends are off-limits." When I don't say anything, he hugs me from behind so we're spooning, which has to be the coziest way to be with a boy. It's like I'm being cradled. "I didn't mean to touch a nerve, Dom. Forgive me?"

"Yeah. . . . I know Amy gives off a certain vibe, but underneath she's the most loyal girl I've ever met. You just haven't spent enough time with her."

"You're right . . . but you don't mind if I'd rather spend time with you, do you?"

Powerless to stop my smile, I roll back toward him. "I guess not."

"Good, 'cause if you'll allow me—" He squirrels under the blanket and kisses my belly. Then he slides his mouth south. "I'd like to try to make it up to you."

16

"You sure are smiley, Dom," Dad observes over lunch the next day on our boat. "So you and that neutron-isolating lab rat had fun?"

"Oh. Yeah. We ordered up pizza and streamed *Saturday Night Live* on his computer," I answer truthfully. Of course I'm omitting everything that happened beforehand, and during the commercials, and afterward until I had to bike home. Mom and Dad aren't stupid, so I'm sure they suspect there's more. But although I'm open with them about how I feel about boys, how far I go is my concern, and I'm sure they're happier not knowing.

"So things are all right?" he presses. "Before that concert Friday, you hadn't mentioned him or cracked a smile all week, so I figured he was out of the picture."

"That doesn't matter now. We're cool."

"And you're sure where he lives is safe? I don't want to think about all the riffraff in those crack shack frat houses."

"Don't spaz, Dad. There's hardly anyone there this summer, anyway."

"So, I suppose you two are an item now." Mom sighs in resignation.

"For your information"—I look pointedly at her—"it's just until I go back to school."

"Oh . . . I didn't realize." She sneaks a glance at Dad. "So you won't be seeing any other boys until then?"

"What 'other boys'? Everyone I meet at the hospital is way too old for me. So as long as I have nothing else going on, it's either Guy or no one."

"Hmm," Dad directs toward Mom. "That sounds a heck of a lot like the path of least resistance, which has to do with physics, if memory serves."

"To me, it's simple math," Mom says back at him. "The time you put toward someone who won't be in your future is the same time lost doing more worthwhile things."

"Like meeting other people?" he asks.

"Yes, or simply pursuing your own interests," she responds.

"Good point." Dad nods pensively while taking a second chicken sandwich. "What do you think, Dom?"

You have to hand it to my parents for disguising their sermonizing as innocent conversing, but I'm dumbfounded they're not more relieved that Guy and I aren't getting serious. Now us *not* getting serious is a liability, too? Is there any way to keep a boy in my life without it being an issue?

When I don't respond, Dad asks, "Why don't you ask this *Guy* guy over to dinner sometime? If you're going to keep running off to see him, we'd be interested in getting a read on him."

"Thanks. I don't know how soon that could happen, though. He works real late." That's also not the whole story, but it sounds nicer than explaining that I'd rather be alone with Guy than share our little free time with anyone else. "*I'm* not even seeing him again until the weekend."

"If that's so," Mom says, "maybe you'll finally have an opportunity to start boxing up your room."

Both my parents have been bugging me nonstop about this since they broke the Gainesville news last week. I'm still getting used to the idea that we're leaving here for good and that I need to pack up my whole life. What I dread most is cleaning out my linen closet and risking another breakdown over the ex bag.

Mom goes on. "Keep in mind, it's a very big job going through all your belongings. You'll want to give yourself plenty of time."

Then Dad adds, "And since those bloodsucking movers charge by the pound, your mom and I are gonna shed a lot of the old crap we don't need anymore. You might want to downsize, too."

"Of course, don't throw out anything you don't want to."

"But be selective in case the new place ends up being smaller."

"So try not to wait till the last minute, Dommie—"

"Guys!" I cut them off before they can make me feel any more claustrophobic. "It's still July, leaving me more than a month, which is plenty of time, *especially* with me having to be in by one-thirty. For right now, though, I want to enjoy my vacation, okay?"

They just squint in disapproval before mercifully changing subjects, but even *that* irritates me, because now they're critiquing the Rauschenberg Gallery. My first week home my parents and I went there to see a show Amy was curating. As if they are in any position to judge.

"I never understood that modern art," Dad states. "And I don't see how there's a market for it. It doesn't look like anything."

"It wasn't my taste, either," Mom agrees. "Most art's too subjective for me. I prefer painting by numbers."

"Guys, those works were *abstract*. They're not supposed to 'look' like anything. It's about what they evoke."

"That's fine," Dad says, "but the only thing they 'evoked' in me is yawns. *I* could've done them."

"At least the hors d'oeuvres were good," Mom concedes.

The longer I'm away at college, the more naive my parents sound when I return. But what breaks the camel's back is when they revert to debating whether mahimahi is better steamed or broiled, which I've heard them bicker over so many times, I could recite their dialogue by rote. I remember Guy complaining that his parents have become uninteresting, and Amy's constantly bemoaning how she and Joel are like an "old married couple" in the bad sense. Is this what they meant? I'm happy my parents still love each other, but suddenly I'm not so sure I'd be happy in their shoes.

"Don't you ever get bored?" I blurt out.

They frown, and Dad says, *"Bored? Of what?"*

"I mean . . . every Sunday you eat the *same* sandwiches made from the *same* leftover roast chicken while you talk about the *same* things that make no difference to the world? I'm just curious—doesn't it ever get really boring?"

Without skipping a beat, Dad retorts, "Dominique, all day I 'make a difference' keeping criminals off the street while Mom 'makes a difference' educating moody teenagers like *someone* I know. And we're about to embark on a big life change a lot of folks our age wouldn't have the guts to go for, so sue us if we like a little sameness in our day."

Score, checkmate, and snap, I think while gaping at Dad. I feel bad that I killed any chance of making this a more pleasant boat trip than last week's, but I'm too proud to apologize. So as they continue talking about the merits of fried catfish, I just chew in silence and go back to pondering what made me "smiley" to begin with: my pro-con list for doing it with Guy.

The obvious pro is Guy's experience. Like I implied to him yesterday, sex with my ex-boyfriend was always a little awkward, as if we were fumbling through the motions of what we thought was right but could never be sure. So it'd be a wasted opportunity not to go for it when I'm finally with someone who's been there, done that, and could teach me a thing or two.

Another pro—although it's more of a fringe benefit since I'd never use this as a reason to go all the way—is that having sex would take the focus off oral sex, which I don't want to do to Guy. After he went down on me last night, he looked really disappointed when I didn't reciprocate, even though he said it was okay. But when I gave blow jobs to my ex, I secretly hated it. What's pleasant about sucking on a stiff, veiny appendage that spurts pee and sperm? It made me nearly retch and gave me a neck ache. Come to think of it, hand jobs weren't very enjoyable, either. And since Guy's not committing to me, I'm even less inclined to perform any "job" on him.

But the biggest pro of going all the way is that my ex will no longer be the last guy I've done it with. I know that shouldn't factor in. But after how anguishing the breakup was, I'd like to strip him of that distinction.

That I'm even thinking this way is a con in itself, though, because I'm positive I wouldn't consider having sex with Guy if I hadn't already had sex beforehand. I always knew I wanted my first time to be with someone I loved and who loved me, which it was . . . but shouldn't I want that for *every* time? I disagree with what Amy said about how once you go all the way, you can't go back to "everything but." But now that I *have* done it, it doesn't seem nearly as big a deal to do it again. That's sort of disturbing, and it shows that I really did give my ex a part of myself I can never get back. I wonder if he also feels like he has given up something by losing his virginity to me. Maybe he feels like he *gained* something. Just because the sexes are equal doesn't mean that sex is.

The other big con is whether having sex could cause me to more than just *like* like Guy. But that could happen even if we don't sleep together. You don't even need to date a boy to dream about marrying him. I suppose that splitting up with my ex might've been easier had we never gone all the way, but I'm not sure if I'd do anything differently. For all its awkwardness, making love with him was also beautiful for the very reason that we were new to it. Sex with Guy would be new, too, though, because it'd be making love *without* the love. *That's* the experiment in all this. Even Amy's never done that.

The bottom line is that abstaining isn't ever a wrong choice. But what made these last two evenings with Guy so sublime was ignoring all the cons and just following my body. I've always played by the rules in the hopes that it'll pay off later, and I don't intend to stop in the long run. But if I'm smart about it, I don't see why I can't have some fun, too.

When Guy calls me later that night after my bratsitting job, I tell him what just last month I couldn't have fathomed saying to any new boy.

"Just so you know, I've been thinking, and if you're agreeable, I'd like for you to be my . . . number two."

"Huh? That sounds nasty."

"Guy! Not in the bathroom sense. I mean"—I speak quietly—"the sex number sense."

"Oh!" I can almost hear him smile. "Well, it's, uh . . . almost ten now. If you come over soon, you can still make it back before curfew. Or do you want me to pick you up?"

"I didn't mean tonight!" I giggle. Guy certainly corroborates the theory that men hit their sexual peak at nineteen. "We still need to talk about a bunch of things like, you know . . . our histories and stuff."

"Um, didn't we just have that talk yesterday?"

"I guess what I mean is, like with those other girls, whether you used protection."

"Of course I did, Dom." He sounds hurt that I'd mention it. "Did you think I didn't?"

"No, but we need to go over this. STDs aren't a joke." I quickly add, "I don't have one."

"That makes two of us. And I *do* have a joke one of the guys told me recently: What's the difference between love and herpes? Herpes is forever!"

He dissolves into laughter, but I think it's depressing how true that must be a lot of the time.

"Guy, this is important. When was the last time you got with someone?"

"I don't know. . . . I guess it was Beta's spring formal, back in April."

"Were you tested afterward?"

"I've never been tested *ever*. Why should I if I've always been safe?"

I'm about to tell him that ideally he should get tested after every partner whether he uses protection or not, but I'm not one to talk, since I haven't gotten around to getting myself tested since my breakup. Instead I move on to the next question. "Have you had the HPV vaccines? I had all mine."

Now I almost hear him cringe. "Yeah, my mom made me get the Gardasil shots back in middle school before I even knew what HPV was."

"How about the hepatitis B vaccine?"

Another pained pause. "Uh-huh."

"Awesome. And I know I don't have to mention this, but if we do it, neither of us can get with anyone else until after I leave. I'll just feel more comfortable that way. I mean, if you'd ever *like* to get with someone else, okay, but then we have to stop what we're doing—"

"I hear what you're saying, Dom, and it's all good. I told you I didn't want to see other girls this summer."

"Okay. And I can get us condoms if you'd like. I live near a CVS."

"Remember where *I* live? The Betas keep an industrial-sized box of Trojans in the lounge, so we'll be covered for a while. And yeah, they're the kind with spermicide."

"Are they too old, though? That stuff has a shelf life."

"We just bought them this year, so they're fine. Jeez. What a guy goes through to get with a future doctor."

"Oh, we're not done yet. There's one last thing about STDs. . . . I totally trust everything you said, but I want us to be a hundred percent positive we're healthy. So, I'd like us to see each other's immunization records and . . . for both of us to get tested . . . for everything."

Guy's quiet for several seconds, except for his angst-ridden breathing. "Well, I can get my records no problem, but what would the tests involve? In my freshman dorm there was a dude with the clap, and to check it out the doctor stuck a Q-tip up his pee hole. I'd rather get hazed again, Dom."

"Don't worry. You just have to give a urine sample for gonorrhea. Same for chlamydia. And a blood test can usually determine HIV, syphilis, the herpes simplex viruses, and hep B and C. The only time you really need to give urethral cultures is when you're already showing symptoms. . . . You there?"

"Yeah, but I'm about to ralph." Guy takes a deep breath. I know he's trying not to sound as aggravated as he is. "Listen, I'm down with being responsible and everything, but I'm *sure* I'm clean. I'm not a fan of needles, either."

"Still, it's the right thing to do. I mean, if you had a

daughter, you'd want her boyfriend to get tested before they did anything, wouldn't you?" When he doesn't answer, I repeat, "Wouldn't you?"

"I don't know. I don't think that way. I'm never having kids."

I hold the phone away from my ear, startled by the certainty in his voice. "Well, having kids isn't for everybody, but . . . you don't think you might want kids even when you're older?"

"No interest. They're time-consuming and expensive, and no matter how good a parent you are, they can still turn out to be screwups."

"Anything worth doing is hard."

"I'm surprised *you'd* want kids, Dom. You're the one who says '*brat*sitting.' "

"Oh. Right," I whisper. "I guess I should probably stop doing that."

Since I was thirteen I've made most of my cash by looking after children in my building, and of course they can be bratty sometimes, but I wouldn't have kept at it if I weren't happy to do it. The best part's been watching them grow and learn over the years, and I'll miss them far more than our apartment when we move. Some scientists hypothesize that having children is the only reason romantic love came about. It kept couples together long enough to mate and see a baby through infancy. I've always wanted kids for myself one day, though I don't know why I assumed Guy would, too. Being childless fits in with his footloose existence. That night at Bantam Beach, Guy said we could always date each other again in the future, but unless he changes his mind about being a dad, this summer really will be the end of the line for us.

"Anyway, we're getting off task here." I shake my head. "I'm sorry, but the tests are nonnegotiable. If you'd rather not, that's your choice, but then we can't—"

"No, it's fine. You know I want you to be cool with everything, so consider it done." He takes another deep breath. "I'll go to Student Health tomorrow, okay?"

"Thanks. That sounds great. And I'll try to get an appointment ASAP, too."

Guy then switches topics to a TED lecture with Stephen Hawking he just watched, and I know we're both relieved this conversation's behind us. I'm proud I made us go through it, though, and I'm glad I handled it over the phone, where Guy's hotness couldn't sidetrack my thinking. I understand now why other people might never bring this stuff up. Talking about sex is the least sexy thing you can do. One of the most convenient things about being with my ex was our mutual virginity. We didn't need to worry about who we'd been with before. Looking back, however, I was wrong not to ask him to get tested anyway. I mean, I still believe he was honest with me about his sexual history, but there's no way to be sure. And now my ex is *my* sexual history. I guess soon Guy will be, too. I wonder how many more penises I'll have inside me in my lifetime.

17

At Lee County Medical the next day I deliver flowers to a new mom whose nurse told me she got pregnant even though she'd been using an IUD. It makes me think back to when Amy was late last year and she worried that one of Joel's condoms might've torn. It turned out to be nothing, but she got so freaked out, she went on the pill as backup so they could virtually eliminate any chance of conception. I'd probably like doing it more if I had that peace of mind, too, so when Guy phones that night, I inform him it's another non-negotiable that we use a second form of birth control. He says he understands but that it's overkill as long as we're careful. I say we can never be too careful, especially now that I know Guy wouldn't be supportive if I accidentally did get pregnant and couldn't bring myself to get an abortion.

Unfortunately, my gynecologist is booked solid through the summer, as is every other gynecologist I call in greater Fort Myers. I'm sure Dr. Braff or the nurses at the hospital could pull strings for me, but I don't want them to know my business. There're plenty of websites where I can order STD testing services and get seen at a local lab the same day. So in case I go that route because I can't meet with an actual doctor, I look into over-the-counter birth control options, like the sponge. Since Guy and I will already be using condoms with spermicide, though, I'd rather not host any more foreign objects inside me. The sponge is just 91 percent effective at best, anyway. There's always the morning-after pill; however, it's really only meant for when you have unexpected, unprotected sex, which Guy and I won't be having. I immediately rule out the withdrawal method, because sperm can still be in the pre-ejaculate fluid, and that could spell disaster if the condom gets a hole. But even if withdrawal were legitimate birth control, I don't want to have to worry about Guy pulling out in time.

I continue calling doctors' offices during my work breaks, to no avail. Then on Wednesday, Guy phones to tell me that he got a Certificate of Vaccination card and all negative STD test results from Student Health. Meanwhile, I'm no closer to a satisfactory contraception solution and am beginning to feel like a tease myself. Finally I decide that I'll go to Planned Parenthood this weekend as a walk-in and just wait there in the hopes that someone will be able to examine me. Later on Wednesday, though, I get a callback from a women's health clinic saying that they had a cancellation for today at four, a full hour after my shift ends. It sounds perfect until the receptionist goes on to clarify that the doctor is a man.

"Oh."

"Is that all right with you, Ms. Baylor?"

"Well . . . there's no one else who can see me?"

"Sorry, not at this time. Would you rather pass?"

"Um . . ."

Normally I look forward to going to the doctor's because it's an up close glimpse into what's in store for me later. But pelvic exams are way more invasive than the typical checkup, so having a male physician will make me especially self-conscious. It'd be stupid to chicken out when this may be my only shot to get an appointment, though, so I answer that I'll be there. And the fact is, XX or XY, an MD is an MD, which I keep repeating to myself in the clinic waiting room that afternoon as I shakily fill out the intake paperwork. My anxiety promptly turns into annoyance when I reach the part that asks for my marital status. Last year at my gynecologist's I contemplated inserting the word "mentally" before "married" and checking that. It seemed ludicrous to check "single" when the very reason I was even getting a pelvic exam was because I was *not* single. Now I want to insert "mentally" before "divorced" and draw in an entirely new box for "summer romance." If I had my own medical practice, I'd have boxes for every possible state, because whichever one you're in can impact your health as much as anything else.

I check the "single" box and complete the rest of the pages, by which time my skin's coated with nervous sweat. At least the physician assistant's a woman.

"Hello. I'm Rosemary," she says while leading me down the hall.

"Hi. I'm Dominique," I say stupidly as if she hadn't just called my name.

First she points me to the bathroom and hands me a cleansing wipe and plastic container for a urine sample. When I come back out, she shows me to the exam room, where she takes my temperature, weight, and blood pressure. Then she says she'll give me a few minutes alone to undress. After she leaves, I strip except for my socks and put on the disposable gown she left me. It's really just a sleeveless robe with the texture of paper towels, and the armholes are so big you can see the sides of my boobs.

"Your pregnancy test came back negative," Rosemary announces upon returning. "And I see from your paperwork that the reason you're here is because you want things to stay that way."

"Yeah." I force a giggle. "I'd like a backup birth control to use with condoms. And also I need to get tested for HIV and everything. I'm okay, but just to be sure."

"That's fine. And results are available in two days."

"Great!" My heart hammers. Friday will be the night!

"Just a few questions. Have you had any major illnesses or surgeries in the past?"

"No. Just my wisdom teeth out when I was fifteen."

"Do you take any medication?"

"Only vitamins."

"Okay. When was your last menstrual period?"

"Sunday. It ended today."

"And your cycle's regular?"

"Pretty much. Earlier this year it got thrown off for a couple months when I was really stressed out, but now it's back to every three and a half to four weeks."

"Any spotting between periods?"

"Almost never. Usually just, you know, clear stuff."

"And you already had the human papillomavirus vaccines?

"Yes. Four years ago."

"That was a healthy choice. It protects you from most types of cervical cancers and genital warts." She looks at my paperwork again. "And from what you wrote here, your last trip to the gynecologist was fourteen months ago?"

"Yes, that's the only other time I've been. My doctor said I wouldn't need to go again this year as long as I felt okay and there were no major changes, but I want tests and a prescription now."

"Are you sexually active?"

"Um, yeah. That's why I began going to the gynecologist's. I know you're supposed to get examined when . . . all of that starts happening." Admitting that I've gone all the way doesn't feel as strange as it did during my first appointment. But it's still bizarre knowing that my non-virginity is part of my medical record, like it's official.

"And do you use protection?"

"Yes. Well . . . I always used condoms for, you know, normal sex. Not that other kinds aren't normal. It's just—"

I blush, recalling Saturday night in Guy's room. I'm usually so cautious, you'd think I would've insisted on him using a dental dam, but it didn't even occur to me until after it was over. Your brain really does turn to mush in the heat of the moment.

"I haven't always used protection for . . . oral sex."

"Just keep in mind you can still contract a variety of sexually transmitted diseases through unprotected oral-genital contact. The same holds true for *outer*course, what we call skin-to-skin genital contact without penetration."

"I understand."

It's time for my blood test, so Rosemary tells me to relax my arm as she ties a tourniquet around the upper part of it and rubs a disinfectant cloth over my inner elbow. She then has me make a fist while she pricks me and draws four vials of blood. Afterward she covers the puncture site with a cotton ball and Band-Aid before taking the vials to the lab, leaving me alone and as tense as ever. I use the time to text Amy, who's just getting out of work.

Amy: You'll be fine. It's a routine exam.
Dominique: I know, but I still can't believe that soon some man I never met will be touching me THERE.
Amy: I know what you mean. On Friday I'll be going through airport security again for Joel. Ah, the indignities we suffer to get nookie!
Dominique: Whatever. I'll take a patdown over a pap smear any day.
Amy: Maybe you'll luck out and your doc will be super old with shaky hands. HAHAHAHA!!!!

I'm typing back "Gross" when the door swings open. Rosemary walks in, along with a man in a white coat, who I presume is my gynecologist. Frantically, I shove my cell back into my purse so they can't see what we're writing.

The man holds out his hand to me. "Hello, Dominique. Nice to meet you. I'm Dr. Mike Monahan."

I hold my gown closed tightly as we shake. He's not old but definitely middle-aged. The fact that he's probably seen thousands of women's vaginas by now puts me a little more at ease. I'm glad Rosemary's here, too. It's common practice for a female assistant to be present with a male gynecologist. For whatever reason, having a second woman in the room helps defuse the weirdness.

"So . . ." He sits down on the roller chair and skims my file for a few moments. "You're thinking about starting the pill to use in conjunction with condoms?"

"Actually, I'd like to start Depo-Provera instead. My schedule can get crazy, and I'd rather just get a shot every three months than have to remember to take a pill at the same time every day."

"That shouldn't be a problem, and since it's within five days of the beginning of your period, the Depo will take effect immediately. However, we still recommend for the first week that you use another form of protection with it. So as long as you use the condoms during that time, there will be very little chance of getting pregnant."

I nod, impressed by how relaxed Dr. Monahan makes me, despite that we're discussing my sex life.

Now he stands up and pulls on a pair of latex gloves. "Let's just make sure everything is okay with your health. We'll start with the breast exam. You can lie back when you're ready."

A moment later I'm reclining while Dr. Monahan's standing next to me by the head of the table. He narrates everything he's going to do before lifting up one side of my gown and doing a visual inspection of my exposed breast to make sure there's no puckering or dimpling of the skin. Next he places his hand on my breast and presses it in a circular motion to check for lumps. Then he squeezes my nipple to see if there's discharge. Finally he pulls the gown back over my breast and repeats everything on my other side. Nothing he does hurts, and amazingly I don't feel embarrassed. That may be because he's doing a good job of distracting me with questions about college.

"You're premed? Good for you! Any idea of which med school you'd want to go to?"

"My dream would be Stanford, but I'm trying not to think about all that right now. I just want to get through organic chem next year."

"I wouldn't be concerned. The biggest hurdle is surviving the first year, which you've already done."

The breast exam's over in twenty seconds, and Dr. Monahan says that everything seems normal. Afterward he sits back on his stool and rolls to the far side of the table. Meanwhile Rosemary drapes over my legs a blanket that's made from the same disposable material as my gown.

"Now," he continues, "I need you to move down all the way to the end of the table and place both feet in the footrests."

I inhale and do as he says, careful to keep my knees closed and the blanket shielding everything from their view for as long as possible.

"All right, Dominique. Next is the external exam. First I'm going to simply look at your vaginal area in search of cysts, redness, swelling, and anything else that shouldn't be there. So whenever you're ready, I need you to open your legs."

I draw another long breath and comply. While nothing about this feels natural, it's a lot less mortifying than I imagined it'd be with him. It helps that Dr. Monahan's tone remains just as blasé as if he were checking under the hood of a car.

"Everything looks healthy and normal."

Then he does something that my former doctor did not do—he asks if I'd like for him to hold a mirror between my legs so I can see everything he's seeing. My curiosity outgunning my eagerness to go home, I say okay. Rosemary then pulls up the blanket and has me sit up on my elbows to give me a full view of the mirror. As Dr. Monahan proceeds to deliver a mini anatomy lesson, I realize that I'm far less familiar with my own privates than with Guy's, and I've seen his only twice! I guess that's to be expected, since girls can't really look at ourselves without a reflection, whereas nothing's hidden with boys. It seems unfair, but there's also something neat about it being shrouded in secrecy.

After that Rosemary covers me again, I lie back down, and the doctor picks up a speculum from the instrument stand. The one my last gynecologist used was metal, but this one is clear and plastic. Otherwise they're identical, having the same shape as a pistol. The cylinder part is divided into two sections, which Dr. Monahan says are called blades, even though they're not sharp at all. They look more like a duck's beak.

"As you know, the speculum goes into your vagina so

we can examine your cervix and birth canal. Rosemary has already warmed the blades with water to make inserting it more comfortable for you. Are you ready?"

"Yes."

When he slides the beak part into my vagina, it feels like inserting a tampon applicator, except bigger. Then I hear a clicking noise, which is Dr. Monahan squeezing the handle to spread the blades apart so he can look inside. Since it's been a while since anything of comparable size has been up there, I already foresaw that this would be a little uncomfortable.

"Does this hurt at all, Dominique?"

"Um, there's more pressure than anything."

He must sense I'm edgy, because he tells me, "You're doing fine. Just try to relax and take some slow, deep breaths."

I do, which helps a lot.

Then he says, "There's no discoloration, no inflammation, no polyps. Still healthy and normal. Next is the pap smear." Dr. Monahan holds up a long cotton swab and says he's going to insert it into my vagina and brush it against my cervix to get a cell sample. "Any pain?" he asks when he's done.

"No. I barely felt it."

"Okay, now I'll be removing the speculum. . . . Done."

I'd be happier about that duck-billed contraption being out of me if it weren't also time for the bimanual, which to me is the most awkward part of the exam. As Dr. Monahan explains, he'll be putting his hand where the speculum just was in order to feel around my ovaries and uterus. So I take a final long breath as he then inserts his second and third fingers into my vagina and presses upward while using his other hand to press downward on my lower belly. It's painless, but I'm relieved when it's all over five seconds later.

"You're okay to go, Dominique," he says while taking off his gloves. "After Rosemary brings the pap sample to the lab, she'll be back to give you the Depo-Provera shot and go over possible side effects. Chances are that the only thing you'll have is some soreness around the injection site. And if there's a problem with your pap smear, which I don't foresee, the office will contact you."

"Great. Thank you, Doctor."

"Of course. And good luck with organic chem. Just don't let it intimidate you. That's half the battle."

Even though I'd bet my life that my STD tests will come back negative, I'm still uneasy waiting to hear. After work Friday I bike to the clinic, and it's the biggest weight off my shoulders when Rosemary tells me the good news. I gleefully fold the results into my pocket next to my immunization records, which I ordered earlier this week from my old pediatrician. As I head back outside, I text Amy that I'm fine and wish her a safe flight to Wichita. Finally, I text Guy.

Dominique: Everything is "taken care of."
Guy: Very cool. Got plans tonight?
Dominique: Yes. Beta house @ 8.
Guy: :) Let's do it.

18

I can't help feeling disappointed when I get to Guy's room that evening. I wasn't expecting him to light candles or scatter rose petals. But I just made myself *infertile* for him, so the least he could've done was make the bed. Instead, he tossed some condoms on the rumpled sheets. Suddenly I miss the plush Sanibel hotel where I had my first time after senior prom. Sure, it was silly blowing so much money on a single night, but it was a once-in-a-lifetime occasion. Tonight is, too, though. It will be my first time after my first love.

Guy and I hand each other our medical papers to look over. He barely glances at mine before returning them to me.

I read his carefully, and after a minute Guy asks worriedly, "It says I'm disease-free, right?"

I grin and return the records to him. "Yeah, you're all clear. Thanks again for doing all this, even if it was 'overkill.'"

"It's okay. Sorry if I sounded like a dick about it before. It actually felt kind of good getting the results back, you know? Now we can just relax."

I nod and lay my purse down on his dresser.

"Hey, Dom." Guy lassos me in with his bath towel and holds me against his chest. "Is anything wrong?"

It's fruitless to explain. Having never been in my place, he can't possibly appreciate the momentousness of this night. Besides, our spartan setting isn't too difficult to ignore in the midst of Guy's naked body. Freshly showered, his skin's glistening like dew. Plus his normally wild hair is wetted down, drawing all the attention to his deep-set eyes, which are fixed on me so fiercely that they seem like sex organs.

He continues, "'Cause if you wanna wait, don't sweat it. We can do other stuff. Or I can show you the *Star Wars* prequels, although they kinda sucked—"

"I know, but I'm okay." I grin again and kick away the empty pizza box that's been sitting in the middle of the floor since we ate from it last weekend. "I'm ready."

The first time we do it, it hurts somewhat, and I have to tell him to stop before he can even come. I think I'm just nervous, considering how long it's been since I last did it. Also, I'm preoccupied with thinking, *I'm having sex again! Take* that, *first love!* Like he'll ever know, or care.

Thankfully, the second time, I'm more into it and have

hardly any pain. But as sensual as Guy is, the sex itself still feels awkward. I suppose thrusting is an inherently comical activity, no matter what the guy's experience level.

"So, what's it like having been laid by six different girls?" I tease him after our third try. "You can count us on two hands!"

"It's cool," he says through a laugh, "but I don't care about that right now. I just want this to start feeling good for you."

"Well, practice makes perfect." I wink.

We decide not to try for four, though, because I'm a little sore now and don't want to push myself. Instead we go out for sashimi and kill the remainder of Friday at a nearby roller rink. Not having worn skates in years, I keep slipping, so to help with my balance, Guy holds my hand. Ironically, that's the most intimate I've felt with him all night.

After biking home just shy of curfew, I stay up until three reading *Cosmo* articles about "great sex" tips, which I test out when Guy and I resume doing it the following afternoon. First I lift my leg up over his shoulder, which supposedly does the trick for a lot of women, but I'm not flexible enough to pull this position off for long. Then next time we do it, Guy tries rubbing my clitoris with his fingers, though it's uncomfortable having his hand wedged between us, and we give up on that quickly too. By evening I'm staring bored up at the ceiling, wondering whether casual sex is worth the hassle or if I suffer from some kind of sexual dysfunction. Or maybe, as with anything, imagining having sex is always going to be better than actually doing it, because in your imagination it's bound to be perfect. But just then, Guy stops, sits back on his knees, and asks, "Dom, you know you can move and stuff, right?"

"Move?" I lift my head off the pillow. "I move all the time."

"Not just your arms and legs but, like, your hips. That's what the other girls did."

"Oh. How'd they do it exactly?"

"Well, everyone had their own thing." He wiggles his pelvis back and forth, side to side, and then around. "And they definitely liked it more."

"All right," I say, my enthusiasm rekindled. "I'll try."

Soon we're at it once again, and now I know why I didn't move before—because I couldn't, at least not easily. It takes work to maneuver with a heavy male midsection sandwiching you against a bed. At one point I do manage to arch my back so Guy's entering me at more of an angle toward my stomach, and immediately I get a kind of hot flash from deep within myself that I've never felt before. I can't take his weight for more than a couple seconds, though, before my back drops flat against the mattress.

"Dammit," I mutter. "I was getting somewhere."

Guy rolls off me and says, "Dom, I really think you should get on top."

"I told you last night I like being on the bottom."

"But obviously that's not cutting it. C'mon. *The* Lilith wouldn't 'lie beneath' Adam. Have you had a bad experience on top or something?"

"No. I've never done it."

"So what's stopping you?"

Because if sex feels awkward, it must *look* awkward, and

as long as we're in the missionary position, I'm largely covered. But then it clicks how I like being concealed for the same reason I like having the room dark. As it turned out, keeping the lights on wasn't that embarrassing. And isn't one of the pros of having sex again to try new things?

"Okay, *Adam*. You win this time." I sit up and command him, "On your back, *stat*!"

Once he reclines, I hold up his penis with my fingers and straddle him before slowly descending on it. Then I just sit there for a moment, our torsos at right angles, taking in this new vantage point. I was certain I'd miss that safe feeling of having Guy's weight on me, but it's liberating not being pegged underneath him. Now the only part of me that's really being touched is my insides, and I can center all my attention on that without distraction.

Guy gently pushes his pelvis upward, so I begin moving with him and then against him at varying speeds and directions. At first I don't care how it feels and just revel in my newfound freedom. It must look like I'm hula-hooping and riding a pogo stick simultaneously. But eventually I arch my back again to see if I can re-create that fiery sensation from before. I do. I keep on moving.

I'm glad the other Betas are far away playing paintball, because when I climax, I couldn't have stayed silent if I'd tried to. The intensity's beyond anything I've ever experienced before with Guy or by myself. My skeleton feels like a tuning fork that's been struck. It actually kind of hurts, but it's in an exquisite way. If love and hate aren't true opposites, perhaps neither are pleasure and pain—if you go far enough in one extreme, it resembles the other. The shriek I let rip certainly doesn't sound like I'm enjoying myself, and the groans I hear on the hospital wards could easily pass for orgasms. Now I understand what Amy meant at IHOP last week when she said sex with Joel made her feel like she was going to die.

When Guy finishes, I'm too keyed up to lie down with him. Instead I bound up from the bed to walk it off around his room.

"You okay?" Guy calls after me, but I don't respond. My brain's like vapor, and tingles continue coursing up and down my legs. Then he switches on his lamp. "Damn, Dom. Are you crying?"

"Hmm? No."

But I brush my fingers across my cheeks, and sure enough, there're tears. My hands are quivering, too. I look back at Guy.

"I came!" I yelp.

"No shit, Sherlock. I could feel it."

"It was like . . . time-slowing, space-curving—"

"Now you're speaking my language."

"So . . . how many other people know about this?"

He cracks up laughing, but I'm not kidding. It's as though I've pledged a secret sorority, and the members are the women who discovered firsthand that sex is about so much more than reproduction or pleasing your partner or trying to get closer to each other. I make a mental note to look into buying one of those internal vibrators Amy mentioned. I'll be damned if a man's my only gateway to feeling this heavenly.

I scamper back to Guy and reach for another condom from his stash under the bed.

"Let's do it again!"

"Whoa, girl." He stops my hands from tearing open the wrapper. "I need a break first. Maybe in twenty minutes."

"Twenty minutes?" I could slap him. "Five! Ten max!"

"Dom, this isn't something we can bargain over. But I assure you, we'll fuck the second I feel capable, okay?"

I huff and slump down next to him, though I'm amused by his choice of words.

"We did just 'fuck,' didn't we?"

"I should say so."

I smile. "This sounds loony, but that felt like my first 'fuck.' I mean, I know it wasn't, but before I never *thought* of it as 'fucking.'"

"I'm not sure how to respond to that, but I'll take it as a compliment."

When we do it again, nothing happens. I'm not discouraged, though, because I know the reason is that I was trying too hard. The next time I'm calmer and just go with it, and it's even better than earlier. The first thing I do afterward is check the date on my phone. In the same way that I'll always remember the anniversary of that April night I began having sex, I know I'll always remember the anniversary of this July night when I began having *good* sex.

By this point Guy and I both need a break, and he pulls me close to him so my head's on his chest. My ex would also hold me like this after we did it, and then we'd tell each other, "I love you." Maybe it's force of habit, but I'm compelled to say something sweet now, too.

"Guy?"

"Yeah?"

"I love fucking you."

He laughs again. "I love fucking you, too."

19

As curfew approaches, the idea of leaving Guy's bed anytime soon seems unconscionable. So I dial home and conveniently forget that I'd promised myself after my last relationship that I'd never again deceive my parents because of a boy.

"The hospital called. It's another staff shortage. They need me to come in right away for the overnight shift . . . and maybe through tomorrow, too. I have extra scrubs there I can change into—"

"But it's the weekend!" Mom peals. "Aren't they exploiting you?"

"It's okay. They haven't asked me to volunteer overtime since the Fourth. And I need to be able to stay awake for long stretches if this is what I'm going to do for a living."

"Well, we'll miss you at fishing," Dad says, "but you should be proud they're turning to you for help. That shows you're doing a good job."

"Very true, Dommie. And at least you're getting plenty of experience!"

"That's for sure."

I also cancel my babysitting gigs this week. I know I promised myself never to do that, either, but I want to maximize my time with Guy. Before long, I lose count of how many times we do it, and all the different ways we try it. It's not always good. But the more we do it, the more I learn what to do to make it good, and the less inhibited I feel instructing *him* about what to do to make it good. But my favorite position is still with me on top, since it allows me the most control. I even start giving Guy head—not because it suddenly feels better, but because I'm thinking of it differently. Down there I'm in the lead, and it's fun making him react to whatever I choose to do to him.

What's freaky is that having all this sex makes me feel similar to when I was in love, but without any of the doubts or longings. It's like I'm the healthiest I've ever been, and that I'm always on the heels of the best workout of my life. My skin's radiant, too—my supervisor asks if I've gotten new makeup, and I'm not even wearing any. And although my internship is no less humdrum, I avidly put my all into each menial project. Amy says I'm in the "sex haze," which sounds about right. All day I'm on a cloud as I look forward to what new flavors of pleasure I'll discover that evening at Guy's.

The only downside of doing it at the Beta house is the Betas. Each night as Guy joins me on the walk of shame back to my bike, whoever we pass in the halls makes obscene noises and hand gestures at us or says things like, "Coming up for air?" and "Did you break the bed?" Guy yells at them to knock it off, and I'm sure they're only trying to be funny, but it's a struggle not to feel cheap. On Wednesday, Guy and I can't even go *into* the Beta house because Bruce accidentally sets off a stink bomb, leaving the whole place reeking of rotten eggs. Guy and I pace around campus trying to think up a plan B.

"What about a motel? We can split it," I suggest, forgetting how I'm short babysitting earnings this week.

"I don't know if we could find anything. I heard something on the radio about there being no available rooms left with some boating trade show in town."

"Oh. Damn boats!" A minute later we're passing the Physical Sciences Complex, and I point to it and whisper eagerly, "We can go to your lab!" I start jumping in place, excited to play out my schoolgirl fantasies of Mr. Chesnoff and me doing it on his office desk.

"It's too risky. The custodial staff works till late, and they have keys to every room."

"C'mon. The whole 'doing it somewhere we might get caught' thing is supposed to be kind of sexy," I say more provocatively than I really mean it . . . I think.

"Dom, screwing in a physics building is just a couple rungs up from whacking off in the library stacks. I'm *not* gonna be that dude."

"Oh, all right. . . . Then how about the other frat houses?

Or the dorms? It's still July, so there must be hundreds of vacant rooms here."

"Sure, but Res-Life keeps them locked to protect them from hornballs like you."

"Ugh! I hate this—trying to figure out places to be alone. It's so high school."

Eventually we get dinner at Big Fish, though I don't do much eating, since I have to keep sitting on my hands to stop myself from groping Guy under the table. Afterward we drive back to Bantam Beach in search of our secluded sand knoll, only to find that it has since been washed away.

Undeterred, I leap up onto Guy, wrap my legs around him, and French him in full view of the other beachgoers. And so begins a cycle of alternately making out and prying ourselves apart just when we're about to commit public indecency. I normally look down on heavy PDA as crass exhibitionism, but now I don't give it a second thought. That's not surprising, considering that my standards have sunk to the level of wanting to rent a seedy motel room.

Later during a "time-out," Guy and I lie down together on the sand to watch the sunset. Instead of drinking in the scenery, though, I'm cursing Bruce's name.

"What was he even thinking? Who in their right mind plays with stink bombs?"

"I guess he had to replace his firecracker fixation with something. He's always been into blowing shit up . . . maybe because he studies supernovas for his major."

"I bet he set it off on purpose, just to cock-block us."

"I *highly* doubt that. Bruce was just being Bruce. And at least he didn't pull this crap over a weekend. Then I'd kick his ass."

"Well, it wouldn't make a difference for *this* weekend, because"—I turn to him and smile coyly —"my parents will be in Gainesville the whole time house-hunting!"

Mom and Dad had asked me to come along on the trip to offer my input, but I'd rather avoid us being stuck in a car together for hours on end when my temper has been short enough with them this summer. Anyhow, I don't see how my input really matters when our new home is going to be more for the two of them than for the three of us.

"So," I continue, "how would you feel about 'sleeping over' at my place on Friday and Saturday?"

Guy smiles back at me. "I think I'd be up for that." But then he says he'll need to leave early on Sunday because *his* parents are coming into town that morning. "It's just a day trip, so they'll be flying back to Atlanta that night. They made me promise that since I wasn't coming home this summer, I'd let them take me out for my birthday."

"Wait . . . your birthday's August third?" I get up and crawl over to him. "I didn't see that coming up on Facebook."

"That's 'cause I don't show it. It's really no big deal to me, Dom. Birthdays are purely chronological milestones. Except for next year, when I hit twenty-one. *That* will be a big-ass party."

"Still, twenty means you're done being a teenager forever! That's a *massive* deal!"

I realize twenty is still young. In only two Decembers, I'll be there myself. But I remember when eighteen sounded ancient, so it seems surreal that in four days I'll be having sex with someone in an entirely different decade of life. For no explicable reason, that thought sends me into an uncontrollable full-body giggling fit.

"What's so funny?" Guy keeps asking, but I'm too loopy to speak. "Breathe, Dom, breathe. . . . Hey, are you crying *again*?"

I shake my head, even as the tears of laughter stream down my cheeks. Finally I manage to utter, "It's nothing. It's just . . . it's just . . . I'm gonna be fucking a twenty-year-old. Aaaaaaah!" I collapse into giggles again.

"Yeah? *And*?"

"I don't know. Everything is just so . . . I can't believe this is me, you know? Because this is so *not* me, but it is, and it's fucking awesome!"

I push Guy down onto the sand and pepper him with kisses, which now feel as unsatisfying as trying to get full on bread crumbs. Then that condom in his wallet flashes in my mind, and I pull back from him. "You know, I've always been too scared to night swim, but the water's still pretty calm. Maybe if we go in just a couple of feet and I sit on your lap or something, we could do it without it looking like we're doing it."

Guy lifts his head from the ground and peers at me like I'm certifiable. "Please tell me you're joking."

I can't tell anymore, I want him so badly. "Well"—I look around—"no one's too close by, and the water would cover us—"

"Dom, there's *no* way I'm exposing my nuts to freakin' jellyfish or whatever else is floating out in there."

"*Fiiiine*, you old fuddy-duddy." I lightly bean him with my purse and turn away. But instead of lying back down, I find myself walking straight into the water. I go up to my calves and sit back on my legs so I'm submerged to my chest. I'm still wearing my shorts and tank.

166

"What the hell are you doing?" Guy yells after me, now up on his feet.

"Getting as close to a cold shower as I can . . . although the motion of the waves isn't helping."

"Holy crap, I created a monster! Dom, this is like the beginning of a bad *Jaws* sequel."

"I'm in shallow water," I respond defiantly. "Anyway, there's never been a shark attack on this beach."

"Yet." But then he starts laughing. "Ah, screw it."

Guy empties his pockets on the sand near my purse and comes in after me. There was never a real possibility we'd have sex. Instead we lie on the shoreline and kiss as the waves wash over us and darkness overtakes the sky.

As it's happening, I have this strange sensation of my mind disengaging from my body and hovering overhead. It's powerless to do anything but watch me experience this flawless movie-like scene straight out of my daydreams when I first met Guy. But unlike those dreams, it's unimportant that Guy's the boy I'm with now. There's a new moon tonight, so I can barely see his face anyway. I'm just so glad I'm with *a* boy, acting as carefree as teenagers are supposed to act, while I still *am* a teenager. Since the Midsummer Night's Rockfest, it's as if I've been compensating for the wild and crazy freshman year I missed out on at college because I was too busy being lovesick.

Soon the water gets choppy, making it feel like we're being battered, so we migrate up the beach face and recline in each other's arms. I'm suddenly exhausted, which I suppose is from my having the most physical week of my life. Guy says he'll keep a lookout if I want to nap, so I let myself doze off on his shoulder.

Our clothes are already dry when I wake up to his phone ringing. It's Bruce calling to say that the stench has finally lifted. Guy says we should go back to his room, since there's still two more hours until I have to be home. It's so idyllic here, I almost don't want to leave. Almost.

I grab my purse and say, "I'll race you to your car!"

Even if Guy didn't have to work late at the lab the next day, I'd still be spending the evening at the Rauschenberg Gallery. Tonight's their annual intern art show, and Amy's Kandinsky-inspired watercolor series is the centerpiece of the exhibit. I told my parents they didn't have to come since they probably wouldn't appreciate most of the works on display, but Dad insisted on leaving the station early, and Mom rescheduled a math tutoring session to be there to support Amy. That would make me feel guilty about my secret houseguest this weekend if I weren't already too excited about it to feel anything else.

The exhibit gets a decent turnout for a Thursday, and Amy's working the room like a pro, chatting up local press and gallery patrons. When it's over, she drives me to an after-party kegger at the same Cape Coral loft we went to on my first night home. Then, when that disbands, I drive her back to her house for a weeknight sleepover. We haven't hung out since Amy returned from her last Kansas trip, and we wanted to see each other while we could before Guy comes to my place tomorrow.

"It's so weird," I tell her after we finish watching *Grease* again. "This movie used to make me tear up at the end. But now I'm kind of mad."

"*Grease* never made me sad *or* mad. It's just a feel-good story."

"Exactly. They expect us to believe everyone will live happily ever after. Now let's forget for a second that most high school relationships are doomed." I point my thumbs at myself. "The only reason Danny and Sandy got together was because they met on a beach and fooled around there all summer. That's not exactly the stuff of lasting connections."

"Still, Danny and Sandy have total staying power."

Doubting my own ears, I respond, "Ames, I thought you'd be the first to say that once the passion wore off, they'd get tired of each other."

"Yeah, but they already made it through almost a whole year together. And even when everyone around them tried to sabotage their relationship, they still found their way back to each other after every breakup. That counts for something."

"Meanwhile, Sandy completely altered her image to be with Danny. You always hated that about her."

"But Danny would've changed for her, too. And Sandy herself said that she wasn't happy with who she was before. Well, now she's happy."

To be funny, I lightly knock my knuckles against Amy's forehead and speak directly into her ear. "Ames? Hello? Are you still in there? Or is this the Jell-O shots talking?"

But then she gives me the most annoyed look I've ever seen her give anyone.

"Sorry," I say, a little jarred that she didn't laugh, "but things were getting kinda sappy there."

"So what? I'm entitled, and once upon a time you were *Miss* Sappy."

"Damn!" I give her a smile. "Things must be going really well with Joel."

"Well—" She looks down and curls her hair around her forefinger. "I haven't made any decisions, but we *are* tossing around the idea of me trying to get a counselor job at his camp next year."

My eyes almost bug out. One of the people at Rauschenberg tonight was a project coordinator from the Boston Museum of Fine Arts, and she kept encouraging Amy to apply to their summer internship program next year. She even offered to write a letter of recommendation to the selection committee. I thought Amy would be all over that.

"But, do you *want* to work at Joel's camp?"

"I wouldn't mind getting paid to give arts and crafts classes. And your mom always says you learn more when you teach, right?"

I'm too speechless even to nod. There's never been a doubt in my mind that Amy loves Joel despite her fidelity phobia. But passing up opportunities she'd ordinarily die for, just so she and Joel can be together all year long, takes it to a much deeper level than I gave her credit for. Even *I* turned down an offer of admission to NYU because I knew Tulane's merit scholarship was a better deal for my head, if not my heart.

I reach out my hand and turn Amy's locket around so the front's facing out. I should be happy for her—she's living what a lot of girls only dream of. But as with the movie, I feel troubled. And it's in a weird, distant way, like it's somebody else's feelings I'm having. Maybe I'm too steeped in the sex haze to think straight. Then again, Amy's like somebody else as well. Last summer no one could've predicted that she'd be the one in a steady relationship. But as long as *Amy's* happy with her choices, like Sandy . . .

"Aw, Ames, that's really awesome," I say finally, trying not to let it sound hollow.

"Again, nothing's definite. It's just something we discussed when I was there."

"Hey, the fact that you discussed it at all is huge. I'm glad you two had a good weekend together."

Amy shrugs. "I only hope it tides me over until Joel comes for Brie-*dzilla*'s big day. Zack and Stefan were looking *so* fine tonight," she says, seeming closer to her usual self. "Anyway." She climbs out of the Papasan chair and sets her alarm. "It's late, and you'd better get some sleep. Lucky you, naughty girl, you're gonna need it tomorrow!"

Amy's not kidding. From the moment Guy appears at my door Friday night, time turns into a blur of hedonism and endorphin highs. We never plan farther than the present moment, we try anything and everything that comes to mind, and I think about nothing except how my body feels. When we're not doing it, we're watching TV or rinsing off in my shower, where we just end up doing it again. I had already stocked the fridge before he came over so there'd be no need to go out or order in delivery. Guy and I don't even wear clothes until Sunday, when I wake up early to cook us brunch. I serve it out on the terrace, the only space in the apartment where we haven't gone all the way in the last thirty-six hours. Normally I would've considered it gross to have sex on my parents' bedroom floor or on the living room love seat, where my parents sit, but with the apartment going on the market soon, no location seems sacred.

"Thank you so much, Dom. This is a great surprise," Guy says after blowing out the birthday candle I planted in the middle of his Belgian waffle, which I adorned with fanned strawberries and powdered sugar. "But you totally didn't have to do all this."

"I know, but I still say twenty is a big deal. And this is fun!"

We begin scarfing down our food much faster than we need to. Neither of us says it, but I know we're both aiming to squeeze in another quickie before he leaves to get his parents at the airport. Then Guy receives a text from Bruce.

"So, Dom." He downs the last strip of turkey bacon while reading from his cell. "That wedding's not this Saturday but the next one, right?"

"Yep. Wow, it's coming up quickly!" I finish the rest of my egg-white omelet. "I need to order their gift soon."

"It looks like the guys wanna go to Disney World that

weekend, kind of as a last hurrah before all the rush crap starts." He spoons some grits. "Is it too late for me to bow out so I can join them?"

I can feel my cheeks drain of blood, and I nearly fling the grits at him. It sucks enough when girlfriends break plans with each other for a boy, but at least that's not against the natural order of things, like when a boy blows off his girl-friend for friends. . . . Or maybe I've had it wrong all along. Since friendships usually outlast relationships, why *shouldn't* friends receive preferential treatment?

Because you don't sleep with your friends!

"Okay, Dom. From that look on your face, it *is* too late to bow out. Forget I said anything." Guy laughs, slurps the rest of his banana-orange smoothie, and begins typing back a text.

I could just let this slide so everything can go on as it has been. The status quo hasn't changed. But suddenly I'm seeth-ing. And after a marathon weekend of never holding back, I wouldn't restrain myself now even if I wanted to.

Before Guy can press SEND, I tell him, "No. Go with your brothers."

"It's fine. I already said I'd go with you."

"Well, *yeah,* but I don't want that to be the reason."

He puts down the phone. "Why wouldn't that be the reason?"

"I want you to go to the wedding because *you* want to go to the wedding."

"I *do* want to go to the wedding. I wouldn't have said yes if I didn't." He spears a cantaloupe slice. "I even got my suit pressed."

"Okay, but now *I* don't want you to go to the wedding."

Guy wrinkles his nose and asks with his mouth full, "Why the hell not?"

"How can I enjoy your being there if I know you'd rather be at Disney World?"

"Dom, of course I'd rather be at Epcot with my buddies than at some church with a bunch of people I'll never see again. Why wouldn't I?"

"Because . . . you'd also be with me."

"I'm with you all the time! Lately I've barely seen my brothers at all."

"Yeah, but it's already August. Three more weeks and *we* may never see each other again, either!"

Guy turns away, and we both fall silent. I feel like we're back on our third date, sparring at Bantam Beach about the state of our relationship. It's sick how you can be intimate with someone one minute and then be furious with that same person the next.

After an interminable lull, Guy says, "Listen, can we just leave this till tonight? I need to pick up my parents soon."

I realize that if he were a real boyfriend, I'd be going with him to meet them.

"That cool, Dom?"

"I guess it'll have to be," I say bitchily, hardly recognizing my own voice. I guess Guy's confounded, too, since he throws up his hands.

"I don't get this. Dom, I told you I'd be happy to stay in town for that wedding. Screw Disney World, okay? I can go anytime. I want to be with you. What more do you want from me?"

The truth is I'm not sure. As dreadful as our Bantam Beach fight was, at least it made sense. We had opposing points of view, and we argued them. But here, I don't know *what* I'm arguing about. I only know that everything feels wrong now. Maybe it's because all this is taking me back to my first night home during Thanksgiving break when my high school boyfriend chose to hang out with his old track teammates rather than being alone with me. That was a completely different situation than this, though. My ex's actions showed that his feelings for me were fading. Guy's feelings have remained constant throughout. . . . Have mine?

"Don't worry about it, Guy. I don't mean to hold you up. You can let yourself out. Happy Birthday."

I jerk our plates away and go back inside toward the kitchen.

"C'mon, Dom, don't be like that. . . . Dom? Dom? Dom!"

I can hear that Guy's following behind me. I just don't realize how closely.

"What?" I squawk, but as I spin around, the plate in my right hand collides straight into his dick.

"OW! FUCK!" Guy cups his groin with his hands and folds to the floor like a slinky. "FUCK! SHIT!"

"Oh, no!"

He keeps swearing as I set down the plates and dart to the freezer for a bag of peas. I try to hand it to him to use as an ice pack, but he bats it away. Then he just lies there in the fetal position, with tears in his eyes.

I kneel down by his bright purple face. I feel terrible that I hurt him. I also feel terrible that a part of me finds this extremely funny. I guess I gave him blue balls after all.

"I'm so sorry, Guy." I stifle my giggles. "Can I do anything?"

He doesn't respond, and he looks so ghastly that I start to worry he may need a doctor. But within the minute he stops sounding like he's going to hyperventilate, and soon his complexion returns to normal. He takes another minute to inch off the ground to a sitting position, and then to his feet. Finally he hobbles toward the foyer, hefts his duffel bag over his shoulder, and turns back to me.

"I'm going to the airport now," he announces in a slight falsetto.

"Go ahead. Again, I feel really bad. Are we . . . okay?"

He makes a face like I just asked the dumbest question on earth, which I guess I did. Then I pose another. "Do you want help to your car?"

"*No!*" His eyes widen fearfully. "Just . . . stay where you are."

"Well . . . when will we talk again? We need to."

"Just let me get through this thing with my parents. Then I'll catch you tonight, okay?"

"Okay. Tonight."

He shuffles out the door.

I have no idea whether we're still "together," whatever that means, not that it really matters this late in the game. And since there's nothing I can do about him now, I just go about washing my bedsheets and trolling the apartment for ripped condom wrappers. When I get to the kitchen, which is littered with the remains of my extravagant brunch spread, I think how Belgian waffles and smoothies are like the morning-after equivalent of candles and rose petals.

Considering all the trouble I put into preparing this feast, it might appear that I have fallen in love with Guy, which I knew from the start was a danger of continuing to see him.

But I'm *not* in love with Guy. I can feel I'm not. I don't even *like* like him as much as I used to, especially ever since he slammed having committed relationships at our age, not to mention parenthood at *any* age. My neuroscience textbook said that sex causes females to get high levels of the hormone oxytocin, which is called the "cuddle chemical" because it bonds you with your partner, inducing you to snuggle, feel safe, and nest. So even if you're not in love, you may behave like you are. I should've foreseen that playing house with Guy all weekend would only feed that delusion.

I continue cleaning the apartment while trying to work out in my mind exactly what happened this morning and what to say to Guy tonight. Then, as I'm taking out the garbage, Dad texts me that he and Mom should be home within the hour. I'd been planning on going fishing with them this afternoon, since I missed three of the last five Sundays, but I can't face them now. As if I weren't already completely thoughtless for not helping them find a new home, now I had to go and use their old home for a fuck-fest.

I end up fleeing to the Braffs. On the way, I recall Amy's news about her maybe spending next summer as a camp counselor with Joel. I assumed my unenthusiastic reaction had to do with Amy not staying true to herself by letting her life revolve around her relationship. But maybe I was mad because, given the choice, I'd switch places with her in a heartbeat.

21

"I came up with a conclusion to my 'experiment,'" I tell Amy while lounging on her Papasan chair. "Sex for sex's sake can be fun, but it's not always fulfilling. Big surprise."

"At least you're *having* sex," Amy says from her easel, where she's painting an acrylic portrait of Matt and Brie for their present. "All weekend Joel's away on a counselors retreat to some marshland with no cell signal, so we can't even sext."

"Guy and I aren't right for each other, but being with him felt so good that I kept wanting him more and more. It gets confusing wanting someone without loving him."

"I don't know—that pretty much describes every hookup I've ever had pre-relationship."

"But it's like I've put my brain on hold these last two weeks so I could concentrate on being sexual. Now there's this disconnect between what I'm feeling deep down and what I'm doing."

"Dom, nothing tragic happened. Your whole motivation for riding the Beta train was to have an adventure and enjoy it while it lasted. Mission accomplished!"

"It was a mistake, though, asking Guy to the wedding again after we got back together. I just thought I'd milk having a boyfriend for all its benefits, you know? I didn't want to get physical with him if we couldn't act like a real couple, too."

"This is why, before Joel, I never limited myself to only one boy toy at a time. Then there's less room to get possessive and cling to a fling."

"Unfortunately, we can't all have throngs of boys banging down our door, Ames. And even if I did, I think I'd still prefer to have just one guy I can be with totally instead of lots of guys I'd be with just partly."

"Personally, I'd prefer a combination of both." Amy sets down her brush and looks back at me. "So, does all this mean you'd like me to tell Brie-*dzilla* you're now going stag?"

I nod. "Even without the whole Disney World thing, I think it would still be better if I fly solo. Otherwise, Guy would be just another ex for someone to ask me about later on."

"Remember, Dom, you don't need a boy to have fun at a stupid wedding. *We'll* be together."

"I know. I was just excited not to be dateless. But what

was I so worried about?" I look over at the portrait, where Amy perfectly captured Brie's self-satisfied smirk. "Like being dateless is really the worst thing in the world."

I'm still at Amy's that night when Guy texts me that he's back at Ford and I can come over if I'd like. Twenty minutes later I'm ringing the Beta house door. I'm expecting things to be tense and weird, so I'm relieved when he greets me with a kiss and says he's glad I'm here.

"So, how was being with your parents?" I ask when we get to his room.

"Bearable, mostly. They were really nice to visit me. But I'm really glad they're gone."

That makes us both laugh, and with the air sufficiently lightened, Guy bites the bullet first.

"So I went over it in my head, and I was an asshole to bring up Disney World. I just wasn't thinking how it'd come off. You know I'd never deliberately hurt you."

I smile. "Of course you didn't mean anything bad, and *I* was the one who was out of line. I should've been nicer about everything, and I'm *so* sorry about, you know—" I waggle my right fist. "But that was an accident."

Guy crosses his legs and nods. "Uh-huh, I blocked out that part. . . . It was a pretty freakin' awesome weekend until then." He grins.

"Yeah, but I don't get to take up all your other weekends, too. You have a whole life separate from me, and I don't want to keep you from spending time with your brothers—you pledged an oath of loyalty to them!"

"That doesn't change that I promised to go with you to that wedding. And I still can."

"No. I want you to get away with your friends. You

haven't had a real vacation all summer. Also, Amy said more people RSVP'd yes than they anticipated, so it'd actually be good if you don't attend, so they can use your seat."

He raises his eyebrows at me. "All right, I'll go to Orlando, but *only* if you're cool with it."

"I am."

I leave out the biggest reason why Guy shouldn't be my wedding date, which is that I have to stop pretending we're something we're not. Saying it would only ruin the mood again.

I set my purse down on his dresser like I always do when I get to his room, except now I pause at the Isaac Newton bobble head.

"If it's true he avoided women, I wonder if he ever missed it." I tap his face. "It must've been so isolating."

"I don't know. Sure, it's extreme, but at least he didn't have to worry about pissing them off."

"Yeah." I laugh. "It's a trade-off."

"Dom," Guy says somberly, "what you said on the terrace about never seeing each other once school starts up . . . that's extreme, too. You know I never wanted *that*."

"But if you're right that we'll always be on different parts of the globe, maybe it's unavoidable."

"Okay, but even if that happens . . . we'll still be, you know, friends, right?"

"Well . . . define 'friends.'"

"Hey, that's *my* line."

"Seriously. A friend can be someone you speak to five times a day or once every five years."

"Or something in between."

"Hmm . . . How about all the other girls you've been with? Are you friends with them?"

Guy bites his lip. "Not all. One girl flat-out told me she could never be just friends with someone she did it with. If I'd known beforehand, I wouldn't have done it with her—well, at least I would've thought twice. I don't get why she was so 'all or nothing' about it."

"It goes back to keeping things equal. Friendship feels really demeaning if one person still likes the other more, which is probably what caused the breakup in the first place. It's such a misnomer that 'boyfriend' and 'girlfriend' have the word 'friend' in them."

"I don't know, Dom. It's screwed up that people who dug each other enough to go out can't at least stay friends afterward."

"Spoken by a true love virgin."

Guy shakes his head. "Anyway, all I'm saying is, I hope we'll be friends. By any definition."

I can't think how to answer him honestly. In the beginning, I wanted his heart. Then I shifted focus to his body. I was never interested in only friendship.

Suddenly the Ford bell tower strikes eleven. I think we're both calculating how that means I don't have to be home for another two and a half hours.

"Wanna watch a movie?" Guy asks.

"Not particularly."

"In the kitchen I have some leftover cake from the restaurant. Like some?"

"Not hungry."

"How about a walk?"

"Too humid."

"Well, we have Ping-Pong downstairs if you're up for a game."

"Not my thing."

Guy fields several other options that I summarily shoot down. Finally I ask him what he'd like to do. "It's your birthday, after all."

"I bet you can guess what my first choice would be, but after everything, I don't want to be the one to suggest it."

"Well, would you even be up for it? How is, um . . ." I lower my gaze to his crotch.

"No permanent damage, I hope. Would *you* be up for it?"

I never would've predicted I'd be in the mood tonight, but I am. Maybe from having done it so much in Guy's room, I've conditioned myself to feel that way when I'm here. Or maybe I want Guy and me to do something to counteract all the negativity from today. Also, Amy once told me that the hottest sex she ever had with Joel was after they argued. In their case, though, the issue was Joel getting upset that Amy let a guy friend pose nude in front of her so she could sketch him for her life drawing class.

I know this isn't me, and I can't keep doing this forever, but as long as I'm here . . .

I smile at Guy. "Well, I suppose we should check you out to see if everything's okay."

I sit on his lap and unzip his fly.

"Dom, you're *positive* you want this?"

"Yes. Tonight, we're *not* friends."

We do it twice. Technically it's good, but make-up sex or not, this morning's reality check makes everything feel off.

In an effort to keep things more strictly sexual than before, I'm constantly thinking to myself how Guy's not so much a boyfriend as an activity partner or a "fuck buddy." I never lean over to kiss him like I normally would. I even throw my head back so I don't have to look at him, abandoning all thought of anything but me. I had assumed before that I could never touch myself in front of anyone else, but sex now kind of feels like I'm just masturbating with a guy. Then afterward, when Guy falls asleep while spooning me, things get bad.

I don't know if it's the weight of his arms, the narrow cinder-block walls, the sickly-green-colored lava lamp, or just the stale frat house air, but I feel like I'm suffocating. Even though there's still time before curfew, I worm my way out of Guy's hold and leave a new Word document on his desktop explaining that I needed to go and didn't want to wake him. I think how we've come full circle since he did the same thing for me at the end of our first date. That makes tonight feel like a *last* date. I'm not sure how I feel about that except that I have to get out of here. I softly close Guy's door behind me without looking back.

22

It seems like I've finally proven myself to my supervisor, because this week she begins allowing me to shadow doctors. Each day I get to observe various medical procedures, and I even sit in on some minor surgeries. But my favorite thing is simply following the physicians as they're making their morning rounds. It's so nice spending extended time with patients, when earlier in the internship, if I saw them at all, it was just to bring them their mail, gifts, or reading materials.

I don't meet up with Guy this week because I have committed to babysitting every evening, and with things picking up at the hospital, there's not much chance to think about him. I do miss him, particularly when I'm in bed for the night. It turns out sex, like love, can be addictive—I actually feel my body going through withdrawal similar to when I cut out soda this year to lose weight. With every passing day, though, I begin yearning increasingly for the nonsexual stuff, like watching *Star Wars* on my terrace, having nerd talks, and especially cooking Guy his over-the-top birthday brunch. Doing things for someone else is what I love most about relationships, even more than having stuff done for me. But what Guy and I have is a non-relationship.

Amy claims that none of this means I can't continue doing it with Guy, and I agree it seems like a pity not to keep enjoying him while I'm still in town. After Sunday night in his room when I all but ran away, though, just the idea of fooling around with him again feels more fake than fun.

Ultimately Guy and I make dinner plans at the sushi restaurant for Friday, when I intend to tell him that I'd like us to stop getting physical, at least for now, while I'm mixed up about everything. I'm not sure how I'm going to explain it to him, not that I owe him any explanation. It'll probably be something to the effect that it wouldn't be *wrong* if we still slept together, but it'd just be wrong *for me*. Before we can meet up, though, my supervisor phones with the news that the hospital is doing an emergency kidney transplant that night and I'll be allowed to watch. When I call to tell Guy, he's as excited for me as I am, and we postpone seeing each other until tomorrow. The operation is easily the coolest thing I've ever witnessed, and I am so happy afterward when the surgeons announce that both the organ donor and recipient are reacting well. I also feel happy for myself. I may not have found the right guy yet, but I have no doubts that I'm on the right career path.

On Saturday, however, I wake up feeling completely wrong. I'm languid and off-kilter, and by the afternoon I have a throbbing headache that the thunderstorm outside isn't helping. So I down a bunch of vitamin C and zinc and cancel with Guy again, this time indefinitely, until I've fought off whatever's the matter with me.

That night I'm struggling to get to sleep, when my cell beeps that I have a text. I figure it's Amy complaining about how bored she was at Brie's bridal shower today.

I was right about Amy being the sender.

> **Joel fucked another girl & I dumped him. Call me if you're up.**

I gasp and read it several more times before I believe my eyes.

"Hey." Amy answers my call in a seemingly tranquil voice. "Long story short, Joel and I were video chatting just now, and then out of nowhere he starts blubbering like a baby about getting wasted at that stupid counselors retreat last weekend, blah, blah, blah. The ho-bag was this CIT named Heather. Could he get more embarrassingly cliché?"

I gasp again. Just yesterday Joel sent Amy a huge orchid bouquet for completing her gallery internship, and I still assumed that if anyone in that relationship was going to stray, it would be her. I guess you can never really tell what's happening between two people.

Amy goes on, "Then he claimed that it didn't mean anything to him, and he wasn't even going to tell me! Too bad for Joel, Heather the ho-bag insisted I had the right to know, and she threatened to e-mail me about it unless he fessed up to me first."

"Wait—so first she screws your boyfriend, and now she's looking out for you? Ugh, I'm gonna barf. You know she's just trying to make trouble."

"Then Joel kept crying about how awful he feels and that he loves me more than ever and to please forgive him. So I was like, 'Why should I tolerate a lying fuckhead of a boyfriend who I can't trust to hold his liquor without banging the closest orifice in proximity?' That's when I signed off. Good riddance to bad garbage."

"Wow, Ames . . . this is so incredibly strong of you. It takes a lot of courage to break up with someone you love, even if there are problems."

"Well, now he's free to be someone else's problem. In the meantime, I'm wiping this mandala clean. As we speak, I'm putting his stupid locket on eBay. Next it's straight to the fireplace to burn all my sketches of him. Then I'm gonna smash that brush holder he made me in pottery class—it never worked well anyway."

"Okay, slow down. You're sure you don't want to save any of that stuff? It's, like, your history."

"Exactly! Out with the old, in with the new! Joel doesn't deserve one square inch of space in *my* closet. And seriously, what was the likelihood of my first real boyfriend being 'the one' anyway?" She pauses for a sigh. "It just blows because at Amherst he was, like, my male BFF, and I thought we were such a good team, way better than Matt and Brie-*dzilla* ever were. Now *she's* the one at a strip club having a bachelorette party. Life's twisted."

"Oh, Ames, I'm so sorry."

"Sorry? For what?" she snaps.

"W-well," I stutter, taken aback by her anger.

"I don't need any sympathy, Dom. Joel's the one losing out."

"Ames, I totally agree! All I meant was it's a shame it had to end like this."

"I'm just relieved this all happened in time for the wedding next week. Matt's Cornell friends are gonna be there, and some of them are *hot*. Now I can actually get with them."

Amy's saying all the right things to show she's okay, and to anyone else it might be convincing. *She* might even be convinced. After a breakup there's a momentary relief that you're free again. But that's quickly eclipsed by all the good memories you had together and the realization that there won't be any more of them. She's in for so much pain. I know.

Amy's mom and stepdad have already left town for a psychology conference in St. Pete tomorrow, so I tell Amy I'm borrowing the station wagon and driving over for a sleepover whether she likes it or not. When I arrive, she insists again that she's all right.

"That's great, Ames, but I still want to keep you company."

"I wasn't planning to be alone long. As soon as I dump Joel's putrid guilt-orchids on the compost pile, we're hitting Chamber and dancing our asses off!"

"Oh . . . Well, it's almost ten, the weather's sucky, and

my head still kinda hurts. I was thinking we'd just raid the fridge and OD on bad reality reruns or something."

"C'mon, Dom. That reeks of a pity party. I need to *have fun*! Pop some Tylenol and suck it up!"

I know not to take any of this personally. That night last month when I hit rock bottom in my bathtub, I just wanted to get out and be among people, too. As Amy's best friend, I should be encouraging her.

A half hour later I'm driving us over Edison Bridge while Amy's applying makeup in front of the visor mirror. She insisted I borrow her clubbing gear of pleather pants and a bright turquoise halter top, which look positively modest compared to her black micromini, fishnet shirt, and red sequined bra. We're quiet for a few moments as Amy draws on her glitter lip pencil and checks e-mail on her phone for the fifth time this car ride. Then, out of the blue, she asks, "Did I ever tell you that Joel was uncircumcised?"

I almost swerve the car into the Caloosahatchee River, I'm so thrown. I want to laugh, but her tone was really solemn.

"Um . . . *no*. You left out that minor detail."

"Well, that's probably because I tried not to think about it. Uncircumcised dicks are disgusting."

I've never seen one myself other than in anatomy books. I never thought they were pretty, but circumcised ones don't hold the monopoly on aesthetics, either. "Well, they're certainly different," I say.

"And hazardous, too! I got a yeast infection *and* a urinary tract infection while Joel and I were together. I bet that wouldn't have happened if he had a regular cock."

"Actually, there shouldn't be a correlation unless he had

bad hygiene or something. A lot of women develop yeasts and UTIs at some point."

As if not hearing me, Amy goes on. "I should've dumped Joel once I saw he was uncut, but I didn't want to be judgmental. I remember thinking, *It's not Joel's fault his parents were too crunchy-granola hippie to get him fixed.* But it *is* Joel's fault. He's an adult. He could've gone to the doctor himself. Why would any self-respecting male not do that?"

I assume that was a rhetorical question, but then she repeats louder, *"Why?"*

"Oh . . . well . . ." *Are we actually having this conversation?* "It could be because circumcision hurts a lot more in adults than newborns, and there's greater risk of complications."

"A little pain's not a good enough reason. Joel's a wimp."

"Or maybe health insurance doesn't cover it. It's usually not medically necessary."

"Then he's cheap, too. A wimpy cheapskate freak."

"Well, it's not exactly freakish. Something like only fifteen percent of men worldwide get circumcised, so Joel's actually in the majority—"

"Jesus, Dom!" She slams the visor mirror shut. *"Whose side are you on?"*

She's never yelled at me like that before, but I tell myself yet again not to take it personally. She's simply besieged with emotions and is unloading it on the nearest warm body. I get that her whole circumcision rant is nothing more than a classic breakup defense mechanism of dwelling on the relationship's bad points. I did the same thing. But recalling how my ex had nasty BO after track practice never made me feel better. It seemed disingenuous to hold things against him that before I readily accepted as the price of love.

"Ames, of course I'm behind you. I didn't mean to defend him. I was only spouting medical trivia."

Apparently still not hearing me, Amy continues, "I mean, I am *awesome*! I'm wicked hot with brains to match and mad talent. Why should I lower myself to put up with a grosser-than-gross pecker?"

"You're right," I respond, just trying to placate her at this point. "Foreskin—*blech*. Who needs it?"

"Exactly! Fuck Joel and his bagel-dog-looking wiener!"

There's another silence as Amy checks her e-mail again. I can practically hear my Biomedical Ethics professor narrating the scene as it unfolds, *Grief stage one: denial.*

"That uncircumcised dickhead," she grumbles. "Why isn't he blowing up my phone begging me to take him back? He should've at least tried to text."

"Maybe he's scared of making you madder."

"Or maybe he's having rebound sex with Heather the ho-bag. I *knew* she was bad news when I met her there. Well, this is what happens when your relationship gets too comfortable and familiar. The guy's destined to get his rocks off with someone shiny and new."

The moment we get to Chamber, Amy slinks to the center of the dance floor, where within seconds she attracts a half dozen guys vying to ride her thigh. I attract one, and as we gyrate our hips against each other, I think how just last weekend I was moving very similarly with somebody else. I waver between feeling disconcerted and pleased by that, though soon I feel nothing but faint from the deafening techno music. I try to endure it, but after two more songs, my eardrums are about to explode. I pull away from my dance dude and tug on Amy's fishnet sleeve four times before she gets that I want her to follow me. Once we're back outside under the awning, she demands to know what my problem is. When I tell her, she's unmoved.

"Of course it's loud. It's a club!"

"Well, my headache came back times ten, and I wasn't comfortable in there anyway. I saw people doing bong hits near the bathroom."

"So, what are you going to do? Tell your *daddy* on them?"

"No. Of course not," I reply calmly, even though I'm starting to get irritated. I never knew she was capable of sounding so mean. "And I hate to be a killjoy, Ames, but I'm just really not feeling well. Can we please bail?"

"I am *not* going home now. No one's offered to buy me a drink yet, and there're major hotties here. Now that I'm free to hump anything that moves, I want to get some action tonight."

"Well, we can try somewhere else, preferably a place that's *not* a drug bust waiting to happen."

"Anyplace else worth going you have to be twenty-one."

"I guess I can wait in the car while you go back in."

"Dom, that's stupid. Why don't you just leave, and I'll find my way back later."

"Ames, I'm not abandoning you here! This isn't exactly in the best neighborhood. What if you can't get a cab? I don't want some strange guy driving you, especially if you're planning to get drunk. Also, my stuff's at your place, and we have only one set of your house keys between us, so how would we—"

"Fine, fine, fine! I swear, for someone who bitches about her parents being annoying, you're sure becoming a lot like them." Amy barrels toward the station wagon without waiting for me.

Soon we're cruising back over Edison Bridge, and Amy's looking straight ahead as if I'm not here. There's no sound except for the engine, the windshield wipers, and an occasional thunderclap. To my horror I realize we're having our first awkward silence ever. I consider pretending nothing is wrong and telling her about the kidney transplant I saw yesterday, but spontaneously going off about organ donations seems too out of place now. So I just keep driving, and because I don't know where else to go, I head back to the Braffs'.

When we pull into her driveway, Amy checks her cell once more. "Well, this was a fun end to a fun day."

"Ames, listen. When I had my big split this winter, I was destroyed, as you remember better than anyone. Except for death and disease, I don't think there's anything worse than a breakup you don't want. But it's like what Dad told me when I was bawling after it happened—you can't have highs without the lows. So I just feel really helpless because I know there's nothing I can say to ease this for you—"

"Dom, hold on." She glowers at me. "What happened to me isn't anything like what happened to you. You got broken up with. *I* broke up with Joel."

"Well, yeah. But what Joel did was a massive betrayal. So either way, the only boys we ever loved broke our hearts—"

"I'm *not* heartbroken, Dom! I'm not! No guy's worth

my tears," she shouts. "Okay, I wasn't expecting it all to go down like it did, but I'm over it. At least, I *was* getting over it at Chamber until you stopped me, *best friend*. Thanks a lot." Her voice breaks.

This whole year Amy has been my shoulder to cry on, so it must feel as confusing to her as it does to me that the tables are turning. I lay my hand over Amy's, but she pulls away.

"And who are you to dispense breakup advice, Dom? That you've finally had a few G-spot Big Os doesn't magically turn you into some guru of moving on. I think your track record shows you suck at it."

"Wait. Excuse me?" I say defensively. This has gone beyond taking things out on me. She's putting me down—another first for us. "Yeah, Ames, it's been a long, hard haul, but I think I'm doing damn well, considering. I kept my scholarship, I have an internship, I started dating again—"

"Please. Perpetual booty calls isn't dating, Domi-*nympho*. What Joel and I have—had—isn't in the same galaxy as you and Guy. And no matter how much of a sex fiend you've become, you're still always thinking about your ex!"

"Not *always*!" I yell. "I'm getting better all the time. And, anyway, how can I *not* think about him? He was a huge part of my life. Just like Joel is forever part of *your* life no matter how many drawings of him you incinerate."

"Well, that's preferable to your hanging on to that stupid ex bag of crap like it was priceless treasures. It's pathetic."

"*I'm* pathetic? *You* flew halfway across the country *twice* to share a chigger-filled sleeping bag with someone you spent all summer wanting to cheat on! And let's not forget the time you tricked Bruce into kissing you! Karma's a bitch, isn't it?"

Amy bolts out of the car into the rain and up the steps to her house.

"Don't even *think* about following me!" she screams before disappearing behind the front door.

23

I don't follow her. I'm too incensed. Who the hell does she think she is? And how have I never seen this side of her before? All these months, Amy acted like a bedrock of support for me when really she thought I was a loser. I put my keys into the ignition to drive away . . . but something tells me to stay put.

Ten minutes later I take my hands off the keys, and I feel I'm cooling off. Amy's words sting, but I think how breakups can bring out the worst in the best people, and part of being upset is mouthing off crap you don't mean. I remember lashing out at my parents in the hours after I got broken up with, which I still feel bad about—I feel bad about a lot of stuff I've said to them—though they never hold it against me. I *would* be a loser if I faulted Amy for a few minutes of lunacy after sharing a friendship that's lasted nearly half our lifetimes.

Another ten minutes later, I'm more puzzled than angry that she hasn't come back out by now, though I have no reason to think she would. We've never seriously argued before, so there's no precedent for what happens next. I'm still in disbelief that this happened at all. But people blow up and make up all the time. It's probably even healthy to clear the air once in a while. . . . So why do I feel like Amy just dumped *me*?

I've been sitting in the car for a half hour now, and any pride I had has been supplanted with worry for Amy. Finally I decide to try her cell, and my stomach sinks when she lets it go to voice mail.

"Hey, Ames. Listen . . . I'm totally sorry for . . . everything. It's late, you had a really rough night, and I can feel I'm running a fever now, so we're both not in our right minds. Anyway, all I want is to be there for you like you've always been for me, so please come out now. Oh, and bring more Tylenol," I add half jokingly to make it sound like everything's normal with us. "Okay, see you soon."

The next twenty minutes feel like twenty years as I wait for Amy to emerge from the house, which she doesn't. Finally I take the umbrella from the backseat, run up the front path, and ring the Braffs' doorbell. When Amy doesn't answer, I use the knocker, and more nothing. Then I walk around the house to try to see her through the windows, but she seems to have gone upstairs. I'm about to forage for stones to toss up at her bedroom window, but I don't want to scare her. Then I recall the crazy outfit I'm wearing and how suspicious this would look to anyone driving by, so I scurry back to the station wagon and resume waiting there like a stalker. I'm also soaked because the wind caused the rain to hit me sideways, rendering my umbrella useless.

Twenty more minutes later it hurts when I swallow. My supervisor warned me I might get sick this summer, since hospitals are paradoxically the easiest places to catch something. I hate to leave Amy like this, but I'm no good to either of us unless I take care of myself. So I record another voice mail imploring her to call and reiterating that I want to help her through this. And since I can't get inside to change into my regular clothes, I have no choice but to drive home in turquoise, pleather, and stilettos. It's a good thing my parents are already asleep when I get there.

By morning the rainstorm has passed, but my temperature's 102, I have the chills, and every muscle in my body aches. My parents forgo their Sunday fishing trip to stay home and take care of me, including bringing in humidifiers and brewing me herbal tea with honey. Being sick is one of the rare times when I let them baby me. I want so much to get their advice about Amy, but as long as no one else knows about last night, it feels more like a bad dream than reality, which I guess means I'm in denial myself. I try to sleep so I won't have to think about anything, but my searing throat's constantly waking me up. Or maybe it's my subconscious prompting me to keep checking my phone to see if Amy called. I didn't realize it was possible to obsess over a girl as much as you can over a boy.

Meanwhile, everyone *but* Amy calls me, starting that night with Guy.

"Aw, that sucks you got the flu. You should order some miso soup from the sushi place."

"That'd be a good idea if I had any sort of appetite."

Then he puts on his sexy voice and describes what he'd do to me if I were in bed with him, which just makes me cringe. There's nothing like feeling like shit to kill your libido.

On Monday, Calvin calls. The last time we spoke, I hadn't even met Guy yet. I'd be more excited to catch up with him if not for the fact that his free time next year will be monopolized by Samantha. On Facebook they continue showing up together in kissy photos at team trivia, which *I* used to go to with Calvin. But with Amy MIA, it's wonderful just hearing from a friend.

"Damn, Coppertone!" he exclaims in response to my scratchy hello. "I *was* gonna give you crap about your promise not to fall off the face of the earth, but it sounds like fate took care of that."

"Yeah. It's been nonstop here, and now it's catching up with me. I'm taking off from my internship all week."

"Well, I'll let you recuperate in peace, but I wanted to give you a heads-up that I'm e-mailing you the essay for my MBA applications. I took a cue from you and banged it out early."

"Oh, that's great. I'll proof it as soon as it doesn't hurt to breathe."

"No rush. We can talk about it when I get you at the airport. You're still flying in a week from this Saturday, right?"

"Yeah, but if you're too . . . busy or whatever to come out, it's cool."

"No way. You can't handle all your baggage by yourself. And it's been eventful here, too. I have tons to fill you in on!"

"Great," I mumble.

On Tuesday, Dr. Braff calls. I'm so desperate for news, my hands shake holding the cell.

"Hi, Dominique," she says barely above a whisper. "Have you been in contact with Amy since this Joel business began?"

"No. I keep calling her but never hear from her. How is she?"

"Clearly not well if she's ignoring both of us. She's usually so outspoken and audacious, but now she's bottling everything up. I'm going to try to talk to her again now."

"When you do, can you ask her to *please* call me tonight?"

"Of course."

She doesn't phone.

On Wednesday, Dr. Braff calls again. She's fighting back tears explaining how Amy left a note saying she's gone away to Wichita but will be home by the weekend. "I have no idea if she and Joel have made up or if they've even spoken. Oh, she just won't confide in me, and I feel responsible. Our whole family's been so wrapped up in Matt getting married, I'm afraid we neglected her."

I always admired the friends-type relationship Amy has with her mom, but obviously that doesn't make getting through boy drama any easier. It's strange hearing Dr. Braff admit weakness, considering that her job is to help people with personal problems get stronger. In some ways therapists have it harder than surgeons, who can often correct the issue with one operation. There's no quick fix for emotional trauma.

On Thursday no one calls, and though my bug's almost gone, I feel sicker than ever. I read a new *Scientific American* article Guy forwarded me on genetic engineering, which mentions how every cell in the human skeleton regenerates within a seven-year period. Amy and I have known each other for eight years, so physically we're largely different people from when we first met. Suddenly I'm frightened that our friendship, like our old cells, has run its course. We might not have become friends if our last names didn't start with a *B*. But what does it *matter* how we became friends? What's important is that we did, and our friendship is one of the most precious things in my life.

I look around my bedroom, which is wallpapered with her artwork and photos of us together. It would take at least ten trash bags to store all my possessions that remind me of her. I just have to hold out until the wedding on Saturday. Then Amy and I will have to see each other, and I can gush to her face about how much I still need her. I'm trying to be patient for it, but powerlessness is the most dismal feeling in the world, and waiting is just powerlessness plus time.

On Friday, Amy calls. Of course it's while I'm showering, so several minutes pass before I find out. Just seeing her name on my cell display propels me to jump in place with jubilation, and before I listen to her voice mail, I already know everything's going to be okay with us. I think, even when I was at my worst, I knew that it would be.

"Hey, Dom. Thanks for all your messages. I'm in Houston on a layover about to take off. I have no right to ask this, but can you pick me up when I land there at noon? I understand if you're not up for it or . . . if you just don't want to. I know I don't deserve it. I can take the LeeTran home. I just can't deal with my parents yet, and . . . I really want to see you and apologize in person. Bye."

I call back right away, but since her flight has already left, it goes straight to voice mail.

"Hey, Ames! Of course I'll come get you! Dad took a cop car to work, so I can borrow the station wagon and wait right outside the terminal. I miss you so much and will see you at twelve!"

It's almost ten now. With all the craziness going on this vacation, I totally spaced on buying Matt and Brie a gift. If I order one online now, they won't receive it by tomorrow unless I pay monster shipping costs, so I decide to use this time to pick one up at the Bell Tower Shops. But first I swing by the Beta house to retrieve my Herophilus biography, which Guy texted me yesterday he had finally finished.

"Can't you hang out for a while?" Guy asks as he hands me the book. "Lab's closed today while the Complex gets a paint job, so I have all morning." He smiles suggestively and leans against his bedpost.

It's tempting, especially after the week I've had. I even feel butterflies in my stomach like when I first met Guy, but I can tell they're more of the back-to-school variety this time. Classes begin in only ten days, and so much needs to get done between now and then. I'm anxious to return to my old routine rather than prolonging the inevitable. I've been doing that long enough.

"I'd really like to, Guy, but I can't."

"That's cool. I'll be back from Disney World on Sunday night, though, if you want to stop by after."

"Well, by then I'll have just one week left here, and I lost a lot of time being sick, and I just don't . . ." I bow my head until he gets the hint.

"Oh . . . okay." He squares his shoulders and crosses his arms. "So . . . this is it, then?"

"I think so," I murmur. "Sorry."

"No, there's nothing to apologize for. Not that it doesn't totally *suck*." He comes up to me and frowns. "Well . . . what can I say, Dom? It was great knowing you. You single-handedly renewed my faith in premeds."

I laugh. "And you definitely raised my opinion of frat boys."

"Remember, you've never been to one of our parties."

Nor will I, I think. We're quiet for a moment. It's kind of sad, though mostly I don't feel anything. Then I play back the last six weeks in my mind, and a wave of gratitude comes over me. "It's been great knowing you, too, Guy. I learned a lot—*Star Wars* . . . sushi . . . *stuff.*"

"That's a winning combination." He laughs. "And speaking of learning, for my last distribution requirement I have to take a life science. After reading your book, I was thinking of signing up for human physiology in the spring."

"You should! It'll be one of the most amazing classes you ever take."

"It'll slaughter my GPA, though. That stuff's never been my strong suit—there's so much memorization."

"Well, if you run into trouble, just hit me up for help."

I don't know which one of us is more surprised I just said

that. Since the Rockfest last month I purposely haven't been thinking of Guy outside the context of summer. But summer's almost over now.

"Really, Dom? You wouldn't mind?"

"Sure. What are friends for?"

Guy grins, and I feel the glow you get only when you give someone something they really want. Who knows if Guy will take me up on it, but that's beside the point. It feels right to leave the door open.

Then Guy replies, "And since you premeds have a physics prerequisite, I can return the favor if you need."

"That'd be good. I'm not taking it till junior year, and by then I'll have forgotten everything they taught us in high school."

Next we're saying goodbye, and I don't hesitate to lean into his chest as his arms envelop me. Hugs are really underrated.

When I finish buying Matt and Brie the duvet cover they registered for at Bed Bath & Beyond, I still have close to an hour and some leftover babysitting money. So I walk over to Jared Jewelers, where I splurge on matching charm bracelets for Amy and me. Then I go to Williams-Sonoma and get Mom and Dad a new filet knife to thank them for looking after me all week, and for tolerating me all summer. I realize gifts don't magically make everything better, but sometimes they communicate things words can't. Finally I stroll leisurely through the center promenade, basking in the breeze and cloudless sky. But as I pass the fountain by the Courtyard Café, I catch sight of someone sitting alone at an outdoor table. My ex-boyfriend.

PART IV

24

I knew all along that coming home this summer would mean risking a run-in with my ex. But no amount of anticipation prepares you for the first time it happens. If breakups are like deaths, then ex sightings are like seeing a ghost: you feel goose bumps, near loss of bladder control, and the sensation of your heart bursting in your throat. The distinction is that the ex is alive.

He doesn't notice me. His gaze remains fixed on his tablet as he takes a swig of iced coffee. Meanwhile my body shifts gears into fight-or-flight, and it's no contest. I face away and motor full steam ahead all the way to the parking lot while somehow managing not to pass out.

When I get into my car, I just sit there, stunned. I have no idea what to do next, or even what to think. Do I drive away? Or should I return and talk to him? Of course, I'm shaking too hard to attempt either right now.

I wish more than anything to run this by Amy. Hoping beyond hope that she's using in-flight Wi-Fi, I take out my phone and log on to IM. She's offline. So with no recourse left, I just ball up behind the wheel to try to calm down and weigh the pros and cons on my own.

No matter what move I make at this point, my brain's forever imprinted with this new memory of him looking handsomer than ever. But by holding tight to my "clean break" policy and tearing out of here now, at least I'm assured nothing else will change. Speaking with him again could just screw things up with us even more. . . . On the other hand, how much more screwed up can things get?

Our breakup conversation ended with me basically telling him to go to hell, not that anyone could blame me, since I'd just been given the boot. Almost eight months later, though, it's still unsettling having that ugliness between us, and staying on bad terms hasn't helped the feelings go away. Time usually heals all wounds, whether it's the flu or a fight. But maybe bad breakups, like bad infections, require intervention or else they'll keep festering.

This isn't about getting closure, which Dr. Braff claims is psychobabble. This isn't about forgiving him, either, though I think I've already begun to. After all, it's not like he stopped loving me on purpose. And this definitely isn't about being friends, although *in theory* I'd like to be friends. Pursuing a friendship would demonstrate that I've accepted that our relationship is gone forever. What he and I had would feel far more worthwhile if we could salvage something positive from the dregs. And in a world where people selflessly donate their organs to patients they don't even know, Guy makes a valid point that it's petty for exes to withhold friendship. But in reality, friendship with my ex would probably resemble our relationship—with me putting in most of the effort. So until I'm completely over what happened with us, I don't want to open myself up to being disappointed again.

None of this means I can't be friend*ly,* though. Also, I'd love for him to see how good I've been looking and that I'm getting along fine without him, which I shouldn't care about, but I do. And with my family moving away soon, we may never have another chance to smooth things over in person. I just need to act quickly if I'm going to catch him before he leaves the café.

But what if I make a fool of myself by saying something dumb or crying or getting the hiccups?

What if I go back and he's there with a girl?

What if I relapse into thinking I could never love anyone else? That'd sabotage all my progress this year.

What if he thinks I want him back? I *would* love the good times back . . .

What if he thinks how glad he is to be rid of me?

"Who gives a fuck what he thinks?" I shout aloud.

And the answer is *me. I* give a fuck. As my first lover and former love of my life, he'll never stop mattering. But if I choose to face him, the reason has to be for *my* benefit, not to try to make him do or say or feel anything. Ultimately, I have no power over what he or any boy thinks of me.

I check my face in the visor mirror and pat off the sweat beads with a tissue. Then I pop a Listerine strip and take a deep breath before heading back into the Bell Tower Shops. My stomach churns harder with each step I retrace down the promenade, and I can't remember ever being so nervous. Or excited. For so long I thought our story was over, but here's a chance to give it a better ending.

He's still sitting by himself, engrossed in whatever he's reading. It's hard to conceive that I'm really, truly beholding the boy who once replaced becoming a doctor as my number one priority in life. But the evidence is all there—that mop of golden hair; that strong cleft chin; his lithe, tall frame; those lips that appear too thin to be kissable (but I can attest otherwise); and of course those electric blue eyes I spent blissful eternities staring into and being adored by, until he stopped adoring me. "High school sweetheart" is such an innocuous-sounding term for something that can tear out your guts.

It's not too late for me to run and hide again. That wouldn't be the wrong decision. Perhaps it's the smarter one. But I keep braving closer until we're just five feet apart. How marvelous it is being this near to him once more, and how devastating that I can't get nearer. Suddenly I get a whiff of his mom's winter fresh detergent on his T-shirt. I close my eyes and inhale, allowing the aroma to take me back to high school. All year I've refused out of spite to utter his name, so it feels alien—and cathartic—to let it finally roll off my tongue.

"Hey, Wes."

He looks up, and now *I'm* the ghost. He jumps to his feet,

and I almost laugh at the fright in his eyes. It's so fortunate I saw him first, that I had those few minutes to steel myself for this moment. Getting dumped is such a loss of control, so gaining any upper hand feels victorious.

"Dom! Wow! Hey!" My ears burn, hearing his voice again. Then he repeats, "Wow!"

"Ditto. It's been a while, huh?"

"You can say that." Wes crosses his arms and gives me the once-over. "Yeah . . . so . . . yeah. Sorry . . . this is . . . such a surprise."

"Yeah, I know. I was just picking up a few things." I jiggle my shopping bags, which I purposely carried back from the car with me. "And there you were, so I figured I'd come over."

He smiles tentatively, but the mood's super awkward, which was inevitable. I bet he's scared I'll chew him out again. So I just smile too, hoping to convey that I have no intention of rehashing the split. It must work, because his shoulders relax a bit and he goes on, "That's crazy odds we both showed up here. I came in from the city just last night. It's my grandparents' sixtieth anniversary tomorrow."

Instantly his cheeks redden. He must also be thinking about all the late evenings we passed at his grandparents' vacant condo. I'm astounded I didn't remember that this weekend was the anniversary, even though I was guest of honor at their anniversary party last August. I was convinced I'd never forget *anything* associated with Wes. That's another victory—beginning to forget.

"Oh, congrats to your grandparents! Sixty—wow, that's a biggie. Is it nice being home?"

Wes winces. "I guess, but after Manhattan and dorm life, anyplace else feels really slow. I was going so stir-crazy at the house, I came here just to get some background noise."

"I can see that, though I like the mellow pace. It's similar to Tulane. So, is your brother in town, too?"

"Soon. He's driving up from Miami tonight. He decided to apply to law school this year, so he's doing a Kaplan class on the LSAT all day."

"Yuck. I have a friend at Tulane who's applying to business school, and he's studying for the GMAT. I can't believe that in just a year and a half I'll be taking the MCAT."

"Yeah. I'm already getting flyers for GRE prep courses, and I'm still recovering from the SATs!"

"I know," I laugh. "Life's become this series of acronymed standardized tests."

We continue chatting politely about college and our families as if the breakup happened to two different people. I quickly discover that being civil comes a lot easier than behaving bitterly, and acting happy for Wes is far more pleasant than pitting us against each other in some bogus happiness competition. The common belief that it takes more muscles to frown than to smile isn't necessarily medically accurate, but it feels true.

The ideal scenario now would be for me to have a "What was I thinking?" revelation, where I feel completely indifferent to Wes and realize I was more in love with *love* than with him. But I know exactly what I was thinking. He's good-looking, good-hearted, intelligent, and funny, and we have a physical chemistry you can't argue away. I still hang on his every word; however, it takes only a couple more minutes before we run out of things to say. That occurred a lot when we were together, though I always chalked it up to my being too slow-witted or ignorant for him. But after all the effortless talks I've since had with Calvin and Guy, it's curious that I was so quick to blame myself.

"Anyway," I say, breaking the lull, "I need to run. I'm actually meeting Amy in a few minutes."

"Oh! Neat." He sounds relieved this will be over soon. So much for him claiming during our breakup that he wanted to stay friends. "Is Braff running track for Auburn?"

"*Amherst.* And yes, she does the three-thousand-meter steeplechase and all the relays."

"Cool."

We both just shift in place. The separation between us is as palpable as a brick wall. I can almost smell the burning ashes of the last flecks of hope I didn't know I had that we'd maybe get back together. It's so evident to me now that just because someone is a great guy doesn't guarantee we'll make a great couple, no matter how much I work at it and want it.

I grip my shopping bags tighter and say, "So, have a nice time at the anniversary party tomorrow."

"Thanks. I will."

"And, you know, good luck this year."

"You too. Not that you'll need it."

"Thanks. Well, take care, Wes."

"So long, Dom."

I flash a grin and walk away.

As I head to my car, I'm elated. I made no mistakes and accomplished everything I set out to. There's no doubt that I came out as the winner of that conversation, though it wasn't

Wes whom I beat. It was the old me that sincerely believed Wes was my one and only. The fact is, he's only one. I'll never stop wondering about him, and I'll still have setbacks. But after trying my hardest all year to go on without him, this is the first time it seems right that my future won't include him.

Then on the drive to the airport, I grow morose. I expected that speaking to him might rope me back into the depression stage of grief, or as Amy would call it, Post-Traumatic Wes Disorder. It's different from before, though. This time, I'm depressed that I'm *not* depressed. That I don't feel upset by us really being over almost trivializes how special and intense our relationship once was. It was just months ago that I couldn't go one minute without aching over Wes, and after a while I suppose I got used to having a broken heart. Maybe I even began to protect it or define myself by it in some strange way. Pain was my tie to a past that a part of me wanted to hold on to. The more I hurt, the more I knew I loved, and that felt like a good thing. So that I'm letting go of the pain means I'm also letting go of the love. My Biomedical Ethics professor never taught us about this bittersweet stage of mourning that follows acceptance—grieving the loss of grief.

I approach the airport terminal, and my spirits lift again as I spot Amy waving to me from the curb. Now welling with joy, I smile and pull up next to her.

25

An hour later Amy and I are at Fort Myers Beach, the site of countless other walk-and-talks over the years. She recounts how Joel eventually did call her to grovel. He also offered to pay for her plane ticket and a motel if Amy would come to Kansas, and he promised to get another counselor to cover for him at camp so he could spend the whole day with her, which is what happened. They passed yesterday in their room fighting, crying, discussing, making love, and holding each other. Then last night, she agreed to get back together with him.

"Joel was so sorry," Amy explains. "I kept telling myself

he was drunk when it happened, so he didn't know what he was doing. Our situation isn't unique, either. Lots of couples deal with cheating and get through it. I of all people should be cool with a one-time slipup. And I was exaggerating before—uncircumcised dicks aren't *that* terrible."

"That's a relief," I say through a laugh as we detour onto the pier.

"But when we went to bed last night, I couldn't sleep. I was still so angry, and nothing felt right. So at two this morning I woke Joel up and told him to cancel his flight here for Matt's wedding because I just knew we weren't going to work. I didn't want him in any of the pictures."

"Wait . . . so it's over?"

She nods. "For good this time. And I wasn't a bitch about it. I can't be. We're gonna have to share a campus and all our art friends for the next three years, so we need to act mature. Ugh. I have a distinct feeling that my painting is about to enter a blue period." We take a seat on a bench.

"Are you certain about this? I'd totally stand by you if you kept going out with him—it's true all couples go through crap."

"Yeah, but it wouldn't be healthy. I can't date him unless I put this behind us, and I know I'd just keep mistrusting him and tormenting him about it. That'd be unfair to both of us. And it's not like I've been a saint, either."

Amy shocks me again by revealing that she never actually wanted to hook up with anyone else this summer. Flirting was the only way she could think to convince herself, and everyone else, that she was still independent and hadn't changed. And contrary to what Amy claimed at the time, those two weekends she visited Joel last month were *her* idea, not his.

"It freaked me out how much I missed Joel, that I was getting so attached to a guy. And seeing the trackies again and how different everything was becoming just made it worse. I felt like I didn't even have my old life to fall back on. The biggest reason I didn't want to stay broken up was I was *scared* being on my own again, which is insane. And now that it has really ended, I feel like this massive failure. I mean, Joel was eleven and a half months of my life! I get that everything's impermanent, but . . . I guess I didn't want him to be."

Amy doubles up onto my lap and bursts into tears. As hard as it is to watch, it's heartening seeing that love can reduce anybody to a puddle, even someone as confident, beautiful, and desired as Amy. Forevermore we'll recall this as the morning she broke up with Joel and I broke up with Guy, except I'm not even close to crying about him. I'm weirdly jealous of Amy for getting hurt, while for me there's just emptiness, like the neutrons Guy researches—no positive or negative charge. It's so true that the price of highs is having lows, and I think now how my idea for a heartbreak vaccine would be terrible. If love is part hate, and pleasure part pain, then eliminating heartbreak would preclude the greatest happiness. As freeing as being with Guy was in many ways, it was constricting in the most important ones. For me, at least, feeling something, even something bad, is better than feeling nothing.

Amy and I stay on the bench all afternoon as she bawls and rails about Joel. I just listen and assure her that everything she's thinking is normal. Then when we finally head back to my car, Amy moans, "I'm such a hot mess. A relationship isn't like air or water or anything." She gestures to the gulf. "I can live without a boy. So why does it feel like I'm going to die?"

"Blame your body. The whole biological purpose of existence is to mate, so from the time we hit puberty, our hormones are demanding us to couple up. Maybe it's basic instinct to feel inadequate if you're single."

"That's what sucks. There's so many more interesting things than guys, but guys are what we spend most of our time talking about."

"I think that's just the way it is, though. No matter what we do, it's always more special if there's a boyfriend to share it with."

"Or a best friend." Amy clasps her new charm bracelet and chokes up again. "I hate myself for everything I said to you Saturday night."

"Yeah? So you really don't think I'm a pathetic nympho-maniac?"

"No!" She cries and laughs at the same time. "If anything, that describes me. At least, the 'pathetic' part still does."

"The hardest thing was not hearing from you all week. I mean, we've always shared everything with each other."

"I know, but I remembered what you went through and how awful it got. I never thought that could happen to me, and when it started to, I went off the deep end. The only way I could deal with it was making everyone else feel as bad as I did. Of course, that just made me feel worse."

I choke up, too. For weeks Amy was right under my nose

struggling with her relationship, and I was too blind to see it. I thought that just because she was in requited love, her life was fine. If I hadn't been so caught up in my own drama, I could've picked up earlier that all her boy-craziness had become one big act, and that her last-minute Kansas trips were signs of trouble. I can't believe how much I allowed myself to lose sight of her.

Amy goes on, "I'm so sorry. You don't ever have to forgive me."

"Hey, I'm just glad you're back home." Then I repeat what Guy said on our second date when we were talking about hazing. "Nothing bonds people more than going through shit together, right?"

"I guess. I just wish you could come with me tonight as I go through the 'shit' that is this rehearsal dinner. It's going to be hard putting on a happy face for everyone."

"Yeah, but I think it'll be good having your family around. Plus, I'll be there tomorrow. And before I forget—" I come to a halt. "Not to keep the subject on boys, but I kinda bumped into one of the trackies this morning. I told him I was going to see you, and he was glad to hear you're still running."

"Well, who was it?"

I smile at her, and all at once every trace of suffering vanishes from her face. I'm glad to be able to give Amy this little reprieve from thinking only about Joel.

"Oh, my God, Dom! Are you *okay*?"

I shrug and grin. "I survived."

"Oh, my God!" she shrieks again. *"Tell me everything!"*

26

There's no denying that Brie makes a gorgeous bride, and Matt looks like the happiest man on earth as she sashays down the aisle. The entire wedding is beautiful and traditional, though I'm not paying too much attention to the details, since my eyes are constantly watching over Amy. Amazingly, she keeps it together throughout the ceremony even while the minister goes off on a tangent about true love, and she's able to wait until everyone's occupied with cocktail hour before escaping to the restroom for a cry. Back in the reception hall, no slow song passes without someone asking Amy to dance, but she insists on staying by my side all evening. As corny as it sounds, I think we both feel like the wedding is a renewal of our own vows of friendship.

On our boat the following day, my parents resemble giddy newlyweds themselves as they rave about our new place in Gainesville, which they're closing on next month. I've only seen pictures so far, but I'm getting excited for them. Mom will love having her own den for whenever she starts grad school, and the house is only a short walk from Dad's office, so he'll never have to fight rush hour again. My bedroom, with its window seat and skylight, looks cozy, too.

As Dad steers us back to the bay, I say, "So if we're moving the boat over Thanksgiving, I guess that means today was my last Sunday fishing trip at home."

"Home is wherever the people you love are," Mom responds. "But yes, it was your last in Fort Myers, unless you come back for Labor Day."

"You're more than welcome to, Dom. Your mom and I have all weekend off."

I think it over, but by then I'll be deep into school mode, and today was already so perfect and stressless that it'd be hard to top as a final memory. So I ask, "Why don't you guys come out to New Orleans instead? You haven't been since you dropped me there last August, and now I know all the best seafood places."

My parents look at each other and shrug.

"Sounds good to me," Mom chimes. "I could use a little vacation after all this house-hunting."

"That's not a bad idea, Dom. But don't worry. If we go, we won't expect *someone* to be in by one-thirty." Dad winks.

After we get home, I finally begin boxing up my room,

and that week my supervisor lets me put in half days at the hospital so I can continue packing in the afternoons. I ask Amy to join me since it'll be a good distraction for her, and we have a lot more fun than I anticipated, unearthing my old things, trying on old clothes, and deciding what to keep, give away, or trash. We're leaving the ex bag for last since I'm still unsure about what to do, and by Friday I decide it simply has too much sentimental value for me to part with. Amy then has the brilliant idea of photographing everything and then throwing it all out. That way I'll always have visual records on my computer if I ever want to look back, but they'll take up no physical space, and I never have to worry about moving them again.

Once we finish snapping all the photos, we bring the salvageable items like the picture frames and mood ring to Goodwill. Afterward Amy cheers me on as I hurl what remains of the bag into the Dumpster behind my building. And since my bedroom now looks like a warehouse, we drive to the Braffs', where we celebrate our singleness with our final sleepover of the summer, complete with vegging out and pigging out until finally conking out following hours of punch-drunk laughing.

The next day is a flurry of goodbye hugs with my parents, proofreads of Calvin's MBA essay, and nonstop turbulence that rules out any napping on the flight to New Orleans. After landing at the airport, I rush to baggage claim to find Calvin, who I don't recognize at first. His bloodshot eyes and dark circles mask his usual exuberance. Evidently he's also going on little sleep, which I attribute to either freshman orientation duties or an all-night romp with Samantha. When I approach him, he weakly knuckles my upper arm and says in a hollow voice, "Hey, Coppertone. Great to see you."

"You too. Thanks so much for coming out, Cal. The dorms must be crazy."

"Oh, yeah. The froshes are freaking out about their roommates. The parents are freaking out about the rooms being too small. The RAs are freaking out about everyone freaking out. It's the same drill every fall. I'm kinda glad it's my last year."

He stares off into space, clearly preoccupied with something, but then the baggage carousel starts up and we concentrate on retrieving my suitcases. It's only after we board the shuttle back to Tulane that I ask if anything's the matter.

"Sorry I'm out of it. I, uh . . ." He rubs the bridge of his nose and peers out the window. "It was a rough night. I'm fresh off a breakup. No one knows yet."

"Oh . . . I'm so sorry, Cal." I'd be lying if I said my selfish side wasn't thrilled to have him to myself again for the time being. That doesn't make me feel any less awful for him, though. He had every excuse to bail on me today. But as generous and selfless as ever, Calvin put his suffering on the back burner to come and help me with my baggage. I'm just glad I'm here so I can help him with his, too. "I had seen online that you were with that RA, Samantha."

"Yeah. It started off as this total whirlwind, but then the weeks passed, and I guess I was getting comfortable. It was only a summer thing to her, though. She says we're too different. I know she's right, but . . ."

"That really sucks, Cal, even if it's for the best."

"Yeah." He turns back at me. "You know, Sam's a natural redhead, too."

"Oh, really? She looked blond."

"She dyes it 'cause she hates it. I never understood why."

"*I* get it. Red's a tough color to live with. You stick out like a sore thumb, you clash with a lot of clothes, and the nicknames reek: Carrot Top, Flame Brain, Ginger-vitis, Fire Crotch—"

"*Coppertone,*" Calvin interjects.

"Well, I never minded *that* one."

All of a sudden Calvin stares straight at me, and I stare back at him. He looks so kind and nonthreatening and cute. We're in the rearmost seat on the shuttle, hidden from the other passengers' view. Outside, the sunset sky is glowing gold and pink, and sharp beams of light cut through the clouds like fans. What a perfect moment for a first kiss.

If this were a Hollywood rom-com, that's exactly what would happen. Calvin would proclaim something like, "I've wanted you for so long." And I'd answer, "It was you, always you." Finally we'd cling to each other as the shuttle levitated, *Grease*-style, off into the sky.

But life's not like that. It's messy, unpredictable, and unfair. Calvin's wonderful, but Amy had it right. I. Don't. Like. Him. That. Way. I want a boyfriend with whom I can have the love I felt with Wes, the passion I had with Guy, and the friendship I share with Calvin. It may take scads more guys, dates, relationships, and breakups before I find someone who feels right, if I ever do, and I realize it won't ever be perfect. But no one, especially Calvin, deserves anything less than being in love *and* being loved just as much in return.

Calvin must know all this, too. He's the first to look away. Then he clears his throat and does a couple of neck rolls, and he sounds more like the old Calvin as he says, "So, enough about my love life. How was your summer?"

I laugh. "That's a loaded question, but it was . . . interesting. By far my craziest summer ever, but not in a bad way. I don't know if I'd change anything about it, though I don't know if I'd do it again, either. There're a lot of new memories, that's for sure."

Calvin looks understandably perplexed. "Um . . . would you care to elaborate?"

"Another time. Right now I just want to think about unpacking and seeing everybody again and starting the semester. Which leads me to your MBA essay . . ."

I pull out my copy from my backpack, and we spend the rest of the ride going over it line by line. I knew it would put Calvin in a happier mood, since most of my comments are praise.

Back at Tulane, Calvin helps wheel my bags to my room, but he can't stick around since he's due at a Res-Life meeting.

"Remember," he tells me, "team trivia's Thursday night."

"I'll be there. And we'll see each other later at that quad mixer." Then I add, "That's a promise."

"Definitely, and, uh . . . hey."

"Hmm?" I look up at him while unzipping my suitcase.

Calvin just stands there in my doorway for a moment. He still appears pretty cut up, which is expected, considering what he's gone through. I want to remind him that he'll always mean a great deal to me, and that we have so much to look forward to, but it's clear from his eyes that everything's understood. Finally he says, "Welcome home, Coppertone," and opens his arms.

I go to him and claim a warm embrace. "It's good to be home, Cal."

Hugs are really underrated.

ACKNOWLEDGMENTS

Heartfelt appreciation to my dedicated editor, Rebecca Short, to my determined agent, Scott Miller, and to my devoted readers, particularly those who've written me such beautiful and inspirational messages—I treasure each one.

DARIA SNADOWSKY is the author of the novel *Anatomy of a Boyfriend*. Her essay "To Sir Anthony, With Love" appears in the anthology *Crush: 26 Real-life Tales of First Love*. Visit Daria at daria-snadowsky.com.

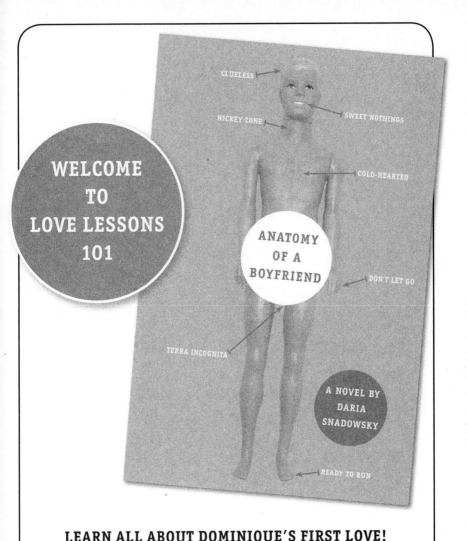

LEARN ALL ABOUT DOMINIQUE'S FIRST LOVE!

Dominique only used to care about the male anatomy
when it showed up in her science textbooks. Then she met
Wes, and everything changed. Crash course, anyone?
If only boyfriends came with instructions . . .

READ & DISCUSS
RandomBuzzers.com

"Snadowsky is as committed to detailing the obsessive emotional character of first love and the excruciating pain of first heartbreak as she is its hormonal expression." —*The Bulletin*

"[An] honest and detailed portrayal of teenage love and lust (think *Forever*)." —HornBookGuide.com

"Snadowsky's first novel is a frank and unashamed look at teenage sexuality and all-consuming first love." —*VOYA*

"This novel . . . deal[s] in modern terms with the real issues of discovering sex for the first time and dealing with it in a responsible way." —*School Library Journal*

"Contemporary teens will enjoy . . . the well-realized, engaging character of Dominique." —*Children's Literature*

"Feelings are intense and emotions heightened, but the love is real." —*Romantic Times*

"Daria Snadowsky does such an amazing job of portraying Dom that I felt like her best friend that she confided everything to." —YABooksCentral.com, five out of five stars

"Snadowsky's writing is sharp, and Dominique's voice is clever, funny and extremely authentic." —TeenReads.com

"Dom's great charm is that she's . . . book-smart—future pre-med even!—but woefully inexperienced. . . . [Her] fascination with biology and obsessive study of anatomy give her explorations an extra-educational kick. . . . Snadowsky capably follows Blume's guiding concept that in literature for young people, the presence of sexual knowledge is far less dangerous than its absence." —*Wichita City Paper*